in control

kyle wright

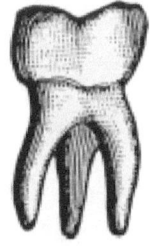

ISBN: 978-1-950305-73-5 (sc)
ISBN: 978-1-950305-74-2 (ebook)

First printing edition: September 24, 2021
Published by Bizarro Pulp Press in the United States of America.
Cover Design by Nicholas Day | Layout by Don Noble
Interior Layout by Scarlett R. Algee
Edited by Nicholas Day

Bizarro Pulp Press, an imprint of JournalStone Publishing
3052 Sassafras Trail
Carbondale, Illinois 62901

Bizarro Pulp Press may be ordered through booksellers or by contacting:
JournalStone | www.journalstone.com

To my family, Dad and B, and Mom, who I wish had been able to hold this book in her hands. This wouldn't be possible without you all.

And to JMP, the love of my life, my best friend, and my biggest collaborator.

in control

prologue

shadows on afternoon. Dark, darkening. Wet street, alive but not crowded. Mist hovers and gets in faces like swarms of gnats. Man in dirty lab coat stands out from crowd. His movements random, counterpoint to the two-way flow, to people on sidewalk. He stops. Looks around as if he's asked a question and no one has responded. Trembling his lips, the question inaudible. We have our own questions, about this man. Until we see the bottle gripped limply at his side. *Oh. That explains it. Another one of those.* A mother pushing her child in a stroller past the man, *mostly* oblivious to him, another drunk, probably homeless. *Probably just wants change or to whisper something creepy to me...*She stops a few yards ahead of the man, lost in a conversation on her phone, attempting to lean over and tie a dangling shoelace. Man with the bottle, Man who might be a drunk, might be a homeless, Man who wears a *dirty lab coat he might've stolen or gotten from the local donation center*, begins spinning. Slowly, dreamily. Eyes closed, arms outstretched. What do we think now? *Oh, another one of those, too. A Jesusfreak, or a drug fiend...great.* The man begins stumbling toward the woman tying her shoe clumsily, phone pinched between her ear and shoulder. Man takes sip from bottle, and we see it has no bottom; just a jagged opening, caked in dry blood. Come to think of it, his hand is covered in speckles of brownish crimson, up the once-white sleeve of the lab coat, cufflink droplets. Man nears the woman. She wipes a blond strand from her face and doesn't see him. He raises the broken bottle like a slasher-movie villain; if this was Hollywood, the sharp glass would glint with a shimmer of light. If this was Hollywood, we'd see a medium shot of just the kid, strapped into the stroller, looking up at the crazed man with the raised glass weapon. If this was Hollywood, someone would grab the man's arm at the last second before he brings it down into the infant's soft face-flesh. If this was Hollywood, someone's beautiful child could not be taken by a dirty piece of broken bottle, right at the beginning of the story...but, this isn't Hollywood.

Which is why, unheroically, unceremoniously, unseen by anyone until it had already happened, Dr. Ross, our man in the dirty lab coat, regains enough of his senses to stop the motion of his arm and the bottle shard before he strikes, and with a horrifying squeal-scream, and all his remaining energy, throws himself directly in the path of an oncoming transit bus. If this were Hollywood, the woman and her child might have been sparred being covered in the gore of the collision, sparred Dr. Ross's blood and pieces of flesh and organs washing over them like whale-water in a splash zone. But they aren't.

chapter 1

like a sweep of light against wet eyes, shimmering city at night. Alternating misty brilliance and mud shadows. The lights of buildings, pin-pricks of life around them, fireflies hovering in little clumps. Take it all in, the way twilight still hangs around the edges of high rises and bodegas with cramped apartments upstairs, banks and turn-of-the-century feats of concrete and brick and glass and metal bones. Take in the way the air smells of car exhaust and trash and wet asphalt. Cooking foodsmells. A group of friends taking refuge from the coming winter air inside a small, hip bar. You can tell it's swank by the trendy sign outside. The friends are all young, well-dressed. They all have nice hair and teeth. Trendy phones, little bits and pieces which signify money, at least a small amount of it. Most of them. Katherine pulls herself further into the cardigan she is wearing, the same one she's had since high school. Sewn holes and removed stains and all. Frail shell just barely held stitched together.

In and out of the conversation, vacuum and lightness. Voices are the stuff of legend in Katherine's mind. Grasp for straws or syllables, pieces of words like confetti around the table. She catches a "Professor Anderson's quizzes..." A chunk of "Did you guys see the Voice last night? I can't believe..." The skip and hop of online jargon, of "for realz" and "lulz." Falter on the cusp of hearing. Almost words and the sounds of voices without their meaning. Signifiers without the signified. It was actually quite liberating, not having to follow anyone else's thought trails but her own, Katherine smiling and nodding occasionally when it seems expected. The others carry the conversation, Katherine just watches and makes shapes in the sand—or in this case stirs the ice around in her drink.

"Did you guys walk out this morning with everyone? My whole class did. Even the professor," E says. Katherine grasps this sentence like a line trailing in the water.

"My professor told us she'd mark anyone who left as absent, even if they came back. Three people still left." Taylor frowns thoughtfully as she says this, pushing the glasses back up her nose

Joey smirks, and his face says he is about to give some rambling, clueless take on the protests, and why they were bad, social justice warrior this, snowflake that, but thankfully is cut-off as the waitress approaches.

"You guys ready for more drinks?" the waitress asks sweetly, appearing next to their table, sweat in the interstices of her hair and forehead. Menus scanned. A Patrón shot for Joey. Whitey has a Moscow Mule. E looks unsure, and when Lan orders her old stand-by, a White Russian, he orders one too. Katherine finds the cheapest drink, a shot of Jim Beam on the rocks. *I guess this is us tonight...*

More long stretches of broken conversation, garbled transmissions, misinterpreted symbols and signs, ghost fragments of small-talk, of familiar terrain, of the same recycled language shuffled into one of so many predetermined patterns of sound and thought. Katherine has trouble keeping focused on the faces, they are sometimes too blurry, sometimes she just knows what they are saying already, how they are moving. Sparkle of the drink in front of her. Amber with little edges of brown and dark, ruddy red. The warm bottom of a river-bed, clay and particulate.

Katherine and Landry huddle in a mass of other shivering bodies, breathing tufts of smoke and breath-vapor. Landry is talking to an older woman next to her about something, Katherine can't pick the noises out from the other voices, the street-sounds, murmur and pop of passing cars, horns in the distance, banging somewhere nearby, the low rumble of music escaping from inside the bar. Her eyes find a shimmer of a puddle and stop, and she tries to drown out the drone of noise by staring into the wet sheen. The way the lights of the bar's neon sign reflect, fuzzy and orange and green, it's a bit hypnotic. Katherine feels her mind sway as she stares.

"Kat? Kat?! You ok?"

She doesn't know how long she has been staring, how long she's been gone. Where she had gone, even.

"Sorry…"

"You ready to head back inside?" Landry asks, tossing her cigarette into a small metal can next to her. Katherine nods at her.

The rest of the group exits the bar, led by Joey, stumbling, sweating the way he did when he did too many shots. The way he did most of the time.

"Ok, guysh. Ordered an Uberk…Ten bucks each. Be here…five minutes." He says other words, but those are the only ones which coalesce into coherence. "Fushcking…Ten bucksh. Ten bucksh."

Everyone begins pulling out their phones and wallets.

"Ven-mo cool, Joey?" Taylor asks, beginning the transaction before even finishing the question.

"Uh-humph. Ten bucksh."

"I'll just…walk," Katherine says meekly. Everyone turns toward her, except Joey, who is trying to get a passing stranger to put in her "Ten bucksh!" for the cab.

"You think that's ok?" Landry asked, taking a long look at Katherine.

"Yeah…it's not that far. I'll be fine." Landry doesn't say anything to this, just lowers her eyebrows in a look Katherine has come to recognize.

"Fine, but if you're going to, use that app we got. Till you get home."

"Are you sure? If you don't have the money, I'm sure we can cover it," Whitney says. Katherine can't tell if its sincere or a smiling dagger.

"No, really, it's cool, I walk everywhere."

The driver pulls in front of the bar and Joe races over to greet the her.

"OK…last chance. Really, don't worry about the money," Landry begins.

"Seriously, Lan, it's fine. I want to do this. What the hell's the point of living in the city if you don't walk around in it, see what's going on? I'll call when I get in the door and throw the deadbolt."

"Ok, just use the app. Like, right now. Start it up. I'll follow you the whole way."

"Fine, starting it up, see? You guys drive safe, or ride safe, or…whatever."

That moment she'd been warned about. That Landry had feared. Her mother always told her gruesome stories about. Her heart beat as fast as she'd ever felt it, rush of instincts, taking everything she had to not begin running as the footsteps stayed behind her around the second corner, too long to be a coincidence. They were following her.

Dark street, a little light from windows or street lamps down a ways, shadows roam here. Keep the pace, don't let them catch up. She looks down at her phone, making sure the app Landry had made her clear space for on her phone was still working; the first time she'd tried it, it had crashed and failed to reboot. But it seemed to be working now.

Her breath ragged pulses, feet on wet pavement echo in the silence, rubber slaps, the soft thudding still behind, not lagging or gaining ground. She didn't dare venture a look, that's when the things could get you, that's when the monsters knew they had won. Teeth like Pennywise the clown, hands scared and green and stretching like that nightmare she'd always had as a kid, eyes like things she'd never even seen on film, wasn't even sure where they were coming from in her head now. Bad pictures.

Not able to help her feet from quickening pace, closing her eyes briefly, overcome with the shapes inside, the ones you can almost poke through, the ones that shift and moan and reach out for you, changing with fever and through the covers pulled over your head, pulling from the backs of your eyelids, like phlegm, like wet wads of tissue paper, like a face pressing into a rubber wall.

Katherine's feet suddenly stop and she wants to scream. Nothing but clasped metal and old dust. Frozen pipes and squeaks. A bursting moment of hot terror and footfalls behind her continue onward, not slowing pace, not even acknowledging Katherine was there, man's face in half shadows. Her breath comes back like a stripped valve. She feels the waver of fast-rushing blood in her limbs begin to slow to a normal pace, her heart bringing the drum-tap back to a more danceable beat. She watches the man as he turns corner and Katherine suddenly feels very foolish. Landry had gotten her all worked up over nothing. And her Mom all those years ago. Always the worst-case scenario, always encountering the smallest percentage. But the most impactful. The most worrisome. Always encountering a possibility.

Lights and honking over her body, Katherine realizes she has stepped off the curb and into the street, in the path of an oncoming Ford Focus. She leaps back onto the sidewalk, the driver never even touching the brake, the silhouette of his extended middle finger the only thing visible in the car as it passes. Katherine squeezes her hands together until they hurt, tries to get her bearings. Something doesn't feel right...it is as if there are eyes on her, but not from anywhere on the street; the feeling is almost coming from...*inside herself*?

chapter 2

a lot of my dreams are the same or similar. I'm in some vast building, a school, or warehouse, or apartment high-rise, always something big, and generic, and unusual. Often, it is either strangely high-tech, or grossly run-down. Some combination of both. I'm always being chased, in these dreams. Nothing particularly urgent, more a vague glimmer of tension in the background noise of them. In the fuzzy edges. These aren't chase dreams, the chase is more a reason for the setting and plot of the dreams to unfold. And I pretty much only remember little snippets—a particular color of printed wall, the light of specific chandeliers, the lips of some stranger or person I had briefly seen in my waking life. Hardly ever the faces, fading quickly as I awake and the washes of chemicals in my brain shift and flow. I can rarely remember the identity of whatever chases me, perhaps it is the same thing or being from dream to dream, I'm not sure. Sometimes, it feels like I'm not really being chased by a thing, exactly...not a tangible thing, anyway. More a...feeling. Like an anxiety or terror pulsing in my chest cavity. In the place where my heart should be. Lack like a black hole. Sometimes, I'll be left with the traces of an outside of a building, seeing the facade as if an establishing shot in a film. And that's about it. I wake up, and it's gone. Like it just dries up.

She never knows how to finish entries in the journal she'd started keeping, it always feels so abrupt, but she seems to just run out of things to write. Should she have some sort of ending? Should she say goodbye to the notebook at each entry's closing?

Her mother's street is quiet, lights pop on as she approaches, the same grey stretch of pocked concrete and the shimmer of glass Katherine has known for years, the same smells: lilac bushes; the McDonald's a block over; the briny smell of the river a mile or two off to the east. Some kind of rubber or chemical factory somewhere nearby she never could quite find. Bodies line the sidewalk, she can almost smell the blood and shit and heavy sour breath hovering, the gun smoke, the carved meat. Sickly scent of death, ripe fruit of broken entrails. Pus and pears. Bile and berries. Sautéed in neon plastic. Wait, *what the fuck*? Katherine shakes her head, trying to wipe away the words fading between synapses. The sudden images. Those weren't hers. Those words weren't hers. Unarmed people shot right here. Those aren't her memories. But she *saw* them. Something, somewhere else. Some *time* else. Gnashing teeth and some kind of glowing eyes, bug's but worse. Sick pit in the bottom of her stomach, threatening to drop out even more, going further down, somewhere outside or below herself. She finds the strength to enter her mother's income-controlled apartment building. To the top. Apartment 4C. Here we go. *We who*? She enters her mother's small apartment and is greeted by the smell of banana bread and the scent of stale cigarettes.

"I can't really stay long..." Katherine offers, hanging her coat on the closet doorknob, an unthinking habit. Her mother had constantly hounded her about this, when she lived there, but now simply waits patiently for a few minutes into their visit before finding a hanger in the closet for the thin jacket. Katherine takes a seat on the couch next to her mother's battered old lazy boy chair. A cat stirs next to her, meowing scratchily before settling back into a sleeping position, his stripped brown fur spreading out across the old fabric.

"Oh, no, that's fine. I'm just glad you stopped by, sweetie." Her mother is looking more her age lately, moving slower, her smile looking a little heavier, a little harder to hold up. She'd started letting the grey patches in her hair grow, take over, giving up the boxed dye kits she'd used for so many years, the chemical burn in the air still vivid for Katherine even now.

Swelling of emotions. Her mother and she had had their ups and downs—God, some of those fights they'd had in high school—but she loved her inexpressibly. Just sitting and thinking of the ammonia burn of those stupid kits brought tears to the edges of her vision, heart beating faster, thumping through her chest and seeming to catch on the lower lip of her collar-bone as it raced upwards and outwards. Shock-waves of happy sadness, little melancholic vibrations, the bitter-sweetness of warm memories, the longing lost time. Maybe using some of it differently.

"You want a cup of coffee or anything?"

"Sure, I'd love one."

Her mother got up and ambled into the kitchen. She was short and cute, almost like a little old lady now, shuffling slowly in her baggy pajama pants. She was wearing the Lil Bub sweatshirt Katherine had given her last Christmas.

Next to Katherine, the cat suddenly sits up, eyes still closed, nose working furiously.

"What's the matter, buddy? Old Man Bubba-cat. Aww, hey buddy, what's up?" Katherine begins talking softly to the cat as she pets him, the touch of his fur running laps in her mind between this moment and her hand on the softness of kitten fur, the softness of youth in her veins, blanketing her skin, Bubba's eyes. Her best friend from seventh grade onward, starting a new school, all the anxious moments before class, not talking to anyone until she made it through that front door. Her hand lingered on bald patches, on scraggly filth-braids wrapped like bad white-boy dreadlocks, wrong and unwanted. He opens his eyes finally, and looks at Katherine for a moment blankly. His body tenses. His fur, what little is left of it, juts out, puffs up as he subconsciously prepares for something he can't quite comprehend, that great question of the wild— that great question of The Clash, should I stay or should I go? Fight of flight? His nose still works in quick rhythm, and he suddenly begins hissing at Katherine. Low growls escape his little mouth, yellow fangs barred, eyes large ink drops. Terry returns with two mugs.

"Bub, stop it. It's Katie, you big dummy. C'mon, cat. You know her. Take a goddamned breath." Terry sets mugs on the squat coffee table and steps toward the enraged animal. She picks him up off the couch and sets him on the floor. He walks away, slowly keeping an eye on Katherine as he does. "He's been a bit funny lately, ya know? I think maybe he's getting kitty dementia or something. He's been...off."

"He is getting old...what, 17? 18?"

"I think so, 17. He's an old man. He's had a good, long life."

"Yep." Katherine picks up her coffee and takes a sip, trying not to think about the inevitability of that statement. Let's just stop talking about it. They'd had to put two other cats down, when Katherine was a kid, and a couple years ago. Katherine knew there was a point when it was cruel not to end their suffering, but that didn't make it any easier. She didn't want to think about it anymore until she had to, until everything was just a little more...stable in her life.

Back onto the street. Colder, darker. A few bundled bodies passing, wads of cloth and half-frozen breath. Katherine feels ice on tears she can't hold back. Trying to get her phone to play music, trying to take her mind off her mother, off her mother's thin fingers holding the scarf, running along it's woolly edges, trying to find a feeling to spark remembering in the brain, her face pinched in confusion, eyes fighting to keep from glossing over, searching. What is this, what do we do with this? It wasn't the first time. Katherine hated desperately to note them, those moments with her mother in the last few years, fearing that cataloging them allowed them to build up. Amplifies their strength. She tries to take *her mind* off her mother's quieting one. Trying not to count time, seconds or steps or breaths or heartbeats. Blocks of sidewalk. Mailboxes or specific cars parked in driveways. It was too easy to lose herself in that, to remove herself from the real with all the numbers and abstractions and compartmentalization. Katherine remembers her brother with dementia, the way he'd slowly grown a large child, uncomprehending in the face of the mounting illness. Becoming the answer trapped on the tip of the tongue. How quickly he went after they finally moved him into a care home—

The fuck? I don't have a brother—I've never had a brother! But such a vivid memory. Katherine has a last linger of the scent of his cologne, something spicy and cool, and then all of it fizzles away. *What the hell was that?* Katherine pulls the scarf around her face more, tucks her hands into her pockets, and presses toward the bus stop. She feels eyes burrowing into her. Or maybe out of her.

Eyes skyward see the metal sheets ceiling so high up. In through the auto doors. This is it. We can still turn back. Run and hide and never return to this place. Katherine presses past a couple of hipsters who have stopped in the middle of the entry-way, nearly blocking it. Keep eyes up, don't make contact with anyone, look for that bird that gets trapped in here sometimes, perching high up on one of the beige pipes running across the open ceiling. Into the crowd. "Is this frozen shrimp vegan?" Let the words skid around your ears, around your face. No eyes no acknowledging anyone. Blinders, blinders, turn up the blinders. "That was the soup that gave Brynlan appendicitis!" Keep walking by. Keep taking sharp breaths, almost to the employee entrance— "If we don't figure out where we're going for our spring trip, we won't be able to start planning our early summer trip!" Scratchy on the sides, ignore the intrusions— "Hello, do you work here—" Nope, you didn't even hear her, just keep going..."Look, Karen, if they don't have grass-fed chickens here, we'll go somewhere else. I know Pear Market has them." Blue puffs of sweater vests. Dust and cardigans and khaki shuffling. Those eyes, dull and piercing at the same time. Look through you and all over every part of you at once. Make you into meat or a monkey wrench or just a pair of hands and flapping lips, take my money, why are these bananas so expensive, cut the flesh this way—

Just get through the doors.

Katherine finds an empty locker and tosses her bag inside. The cold, brownish-grey concrete of the employee backroom always made her a little sick to her stomach, a little dizzy. A muffled announcement for someone to take the call in "Seafood" sounds a third time. Katherine finds a coat that didn't smell like old armpits, and braces herself as she pushes through the door into the Bakery's prep area. She hears the noises of the bread slicer, voices melding together, smells the thick waft of chocolate chip cookies which now only makes her more nauseous. She steps onto the 'floor,' to find tiny Sara sweating and obviously flustered, attempting to navigate the temperamental slicer for a customer's requested half-dozen loaves. Katherine takes her place behind the counter, smiling at an elderly woman who simply continues scowling back at her.

"Have you been helped yet?" Katherine's smile is fresh, false, applied with so much practice she doesn't even feel it pull across her face at the start of her shift anymore. The pinching of her cheeks, drawing the muscles at the sides of her jaws taught. Just after she makes it out the front door at the end of the night, sometimes she feels it sag back into a pinched wince, a scowl, a dead-tired look of desperation. Her face.

"Do I look like I have? I have a cake order to pick up."

"Ok, no worries." It starts. "What's the name?"

"Oh, well, I don't remember what the hell kind of cake you all called it, it was just chocolate and chocolate frosting!"

"I mean, what name was the cake order placed under?"

"Oh, uh...Wellington. Kathy Wellington."

"All right, I'll go grab that for you."

Katherine counts the seconds, trying to gauge just how much extra time she can milk out of this visit to the walk-in cooler. She had found the cake quickly, but the cold and the creepy-quiet are preferred to the onslaught of customers. As she counts upwards, something passes the corner of her eye, a shape. She spins to look; nothing. And there is nowhere to hide in the open room. Katherine shakes off the strange feeling she suddenly has, and pushes her way out of the cooler. Iris walks in from the locker area, still pulling her white jacket on.

"How are you even later than I was today?" Katherine asks, smiling.

"Don't ask me. How is it out there?"

Sara comes around the corner with four bags of bagels and the dull bagel cutter. She looks at Iris, eyes wide, features pulled into pain or terror, it's hard to tell which, and whispers: "Welcome to Hell."

"Great," Iris says, following Katherine out onto the floor. Katherine sets the box on the counter in front of the customer, and opens it to show her. The woman looks at it silently for a moment and, somehow, her scowl intensifies.

"This isn't what I expected."

"Oh, um, is something wrong with it?" Katherine asks, trying her best to convey concern in her voice over the irritation.

"I just...I just expected it to be...to look better, I guess."

Katherine makes a noise somewhere between 'Huh' and a scoff.

"Who decorates these cakes?"

"Oh, well we have a number of decorators—"

"All of these," the woman cuts Katherine off, motioning at the cakes in the display case, "Who decorates them? Because they all just look...terrible! All of them! When I ordered, I thought you'd have someone who actually knew what they were doing decorate it. I mean, did you decorate it? Because it sure looks like it was just thrown together, like the rest of these cakes. I pay all this money for—"

Iris, who has been fixing the bagel display and listening in on the interaction, slams the cake box closed, stopping the woman mid-sentence. Iris pushes the box toward her.

"Have a nice day!" Iris flashes a large, visibly fake smile. "I can help whoever is next, please!"

The old woman huffs once, twice, tries to pierce Iris and Katherine with dagger-eyes, and finally just grabs her cake and waddles off in a fury.

"Thanks," Katherine says, shaken.

"No problem. I mean, the fuck, lady? Who says that?"

Time rushes or crawls, spasms between the two. Bright lights from above. The same shitty Tom Petty song. It wasn't even a shitty song, really; Tom Petty reminded Katherine of her father, who'd play the greatest hits cassette tape in his car whenever the two of them drove around together. It was just Katherine heard it every time she worked, and thinking back on it, it seemed like she had at all of the jobs she'd had. The ice cream stand played 'classic rock' all day, it crept in, even on her off days, even with lots of places to run to. But not when the damn song was stuck in her head. Some desperate moment, there inside her mind. The same desperate moment over and over. Becoming rather a mood than a moment, a nagging cloud than a music. Like crashing waves, like cars rolling by her window at night.

Why can't she just stay in this tub forever? Everything feels better beneath the bubble-foam and the warmth. A safety envelopes her, calming. Steady pressure, like a touch across the expanse of her exposed skin, her tired legs, rolling around her hips, up along the tense muscles of her shoulders. She holds a long thin metal clip in one hand, a small nub clamped between its alligator jaws throwing off a little wisp of smoke streaming up toward the ceiling. The bathroom light is off, candles glowing softly all around, throwing a soothing orange radiance around the small room. Waving in syncopation with the soft motion of the water in the bathtub. Katherine brings the clip to her face, draws on the small smoking nib, her features colored an even deeper shade of orange by the glowing tip. Katherine closes her eyes, and lays back into the water, the bubbles rolling up and over her shoulders and neck as she sinks in deeper. She takes another long draw, and opens her eyes.

On the floor, next to the tub, Katherine sees the dancing and slithering of a snake as it coils toward her. Red, yellow, black, the thick wet-looking animal streaks toward her with surprising speed. Instinctively, Katherine blinks, and when she opens her eyes again, the snake is nothing more than a tangled phone cord. Motionless, limp. But it had looked so real. She rubs her eyes hard, and opens them; before her is a dark shape, faceless, tall and thick and definitely male. Stopped, breathless, tottering on the edge of the light, living shadow. Something in the figure's hand squirms. The figure steps toward Katherine, still impossibly covered in shadows even wading through the candle's light, Katherine can just make out it was a man, not much else, he kind of looks like her old gym teacher, Mr. Brooks, or her childhood best friend's dad, or Burt Reynolds. The man raises his hand and tosses the squirming shape toward Katherine, who instinctively flinches. In the moment her eyes flick closed, she sees a million possibilities of what is hurtling toward her. She hears the splash of something landing in the tub, feels the chaotic thrashing of water moving, of little limbs flailing in all directions. Maybe tentacles, maybe razor fingers, maybe it is some kind of fish with teeth or baby reptile. Maybe it was poisonous. Maybe it was a small cat or child. Maybe it was—

Katherine opens her eyes to face whatever is in the tub with her, whoever this faceless attacker is, and she sees an empty bathroom. Candle flames sway gently as if a quick breeze has come and gone, but nothing more. The water in the tub with Katherine is empty, but agitated into a slight frenzy, colliding in little ripples and waves. Katherine's heart begins to slow, she can suddenly hear her own ragged breathing. *What the fuck was that?*

chapter 3

"so, what are these?" Tone all wrong, Katherine knows this won't end well. She is beginning to be able to tell the trouble customers by how they speak. Katherine looks mutely at the woman for a moment, then at the large sign next to the cake the woman is pointing at that reads "Mixed Fruit Cheesecake." The bakery is nearly empty, except for the woman, who has been slowly inspecting the tables for the last twenty or so minutes. Katherine sighs, quietly.

"That's the 'Mixed Fruit Cheesecake'," Katherine finally answers.

"And that's the only cheesecake you have?" The woman crosses her arms.

"Yes...well, actually, we have bite-sized pieces of the same cheesecake."

"But it's still the same cheesecake?"

"Uh, yes, it's—"

"—No. I wish you still had the old cheesecake. That one tasted so much better. This new one, it's...it's kind of disgusting, isn't it? I mean, c'mon. Do you make this one in-house?"

"Uh, no, it's one of the cakes we order-in, just because I guess it was difficult to make in-house—" Katherine begins, but the woman cuts her off.

"—No, cheesecake is very easy to make." The woman is oblivious to Katherine as she says this, looking over the other cakes in the case. Katherine's face goes beet-colored. Her arms begin shaking, involuntarily curling fingers into fists, all the training of one year of 4th-grade Karate classes, the Power Ranger episodes with friends, the near run-ins with the catty cliques at each new school she found herself in throughout middle and high school, drawing into balls of fingerflesh and dewy palms.

"I'm sorry, ma'am, this is what we have now. I just know what they tell me, and my boss told us it wasn't feasible to continue producing it in-house." Katherine is letting the bureaucracy of her words mask the anger, mask the disgust at this woman. Katherine had been better able to cope with things like this, when she first started. But slowly, when it happened every third customer, and when Katherine saw how her managers not only allowed this behavior, but rewarded it with apologies and free compensation for the customer's "troubles"— A name spelled incorrectly on the cake from specific directions given by said customer, or fruit which wasn't shiny enough, or bread which was just 'too done on the bottom,' though the customer found it sensible to keep attempting to purchase another loaf each week, so many more and far worse instances that Katherine has blocked them from her memory to protect what little sanity she is left with. Now, each interaction is a dam with cracks. An old balloon, sagging rubber flesh, thin and ready to pop with little provocation.

"Well, I think that is a lie, and I do not like to be lied to. What is your name, miss, because I am done speaking to an idiot counter-jockey who can't even do her job when it's frickin' baking bread at All Foods!"

Those clichés about broken camels, about straws and backs snapping, they click suddenly into place in Katherine's mind. She suddenly needs her body to hurt, to maim. She needs the feel and sight and smell of blood. Perhaps the taste of it. What movements does one make, precisely? Only in one playground fight, 8 or 9 years old, a couple pushes from both parties and the recess ladies had broken it up, nothing more. Had movies and television given her body a language she could put to use to express the hot rage she felt surging through her? The intensity of all her flesh and organs tensing, balling, turning her into one large fist. Had video games prepared her? She wants to melt this woman, to Hulk-press her into a ball of mush, to create a blood tizzy, she wants to lay this woman's entire family on the alter for sacrifice.

Hoping for instinct to grab the reins, she leaps forward over the counter, her hand grasping one of the metal cake-stands as she does, pulling it with her. Across the counter in one smooth motion. The woman's face registers shock, just before Katherine brings the cake-stand down, pure instinct, into the woman's thin blonde head—

Katherine suddenly feels sick, behind the counter, realizing the woman is staring at her awaiting a response. The screams, the blood, the feel of the cake stand as it hit scalp—it all felt so real. *Too real*, she thinks. Katherine stumbles away, trying to hold back a dry heave which feels as if it might not be so dry. The woman opens her mouth as if to say something further, hesitates. Iris approaches quickly.

"So, did you need that cheesecake boxed up for you today?" Iris's patented big fake smile as the woman scowls at Katherine's back disappearing into the bakery prep area.

"Oh...um, er, yes, I guess so."

She lost herself on the way to class. The quick bus ride, having a strange urge to lick the finger-printed window and attributing it to fatigue. Suddenly, she is staring at the campus police office, two officers moving around lazily inside, shuffling papers, guns holstered, a strange detail Katherine realizes she is focused on. Why? Is she frightened? How did she end up here, her class is almost across campus and she is already running late? Something in her stomach lurches a little as she pulls herself away from the glass building. A tiny voice in the back of her mind whispers *you wanted to see them pull those guns. Lusted after it. You wanted to hear the explosion when they went off, didn't you?*

"No," she says out loud to the passing bushes and old brick buildings. Something about speaking aloud proves to her that voice wasn't hers.

"Mine sounds like this," she speaks, again. A laughter grows from inside, and Katherine can't tell where her voice fits within it. Frightened, she quickens her pace toward class.

The laughter started first, that day in the old classroom. Little squelched giggles, choking, squeezed hilarity held in-check. Then the whispers. Katherine looks around at the others in the classroom. They are all silently listening to the professor drone on about base units and perfect material balance. It seems they don't hear any of this. The laughter begins busting loose, stereophonic pockets of it, Katherine can't place where in the room it is coming from; *who* is it coming from. All four corners of the room at once, the walls and the ceiling. Katherine's fellow students sit silent, close-mouthed, sullen. The whispers begin growing to chatter. Garbled words just making the noise of talking, like the gibberish writing on a puppy's newspaper chew toy pretending to be real words. Then, the movement begins, and Katherine pinpoints where the noises are coming from. When she sees it, she sits bolt upright. Every fiber of her body tenses, shimmers with cold fear. The walls. All of the weird taxidermy and creepy sciencey stuff on the walls. The deer head moves first. The jaws begin juddering, the black lips curling in a dry, cracked sneer. The laughter continues. The other things hung grotesquely to the wall begin to move as well. Flapping of wings, the rolling of black glass eyes, the laughter and the chatter. Katherine hears her name as one of the only words discernible through the noise. Other things on the wall begin flapping as well, posters, mineral samples, Dinosaur bone models, the bisected human heart begins pumping and spurting blood, dribbling lumpy brown-red streaks down the wall. The laughing becomes shrieking, the animals thrash and flail as if they are trying to work themselves off their mounts. Foam and blood and the awful noises all around her. Katherine's classmates still bored to tears by the professor, but oblivious to the noise and movement coming from the walls around them. Katherine closes her eyes but the roar continues. It is almost as if it has moved into her head. Ricocheting off her closed eyelids. She has to leave. She can't take any more of this. Katherine stands and grabs her bag. As she reaches the door, all eyes in the classroom burning into her back, the deer head turned downward to continue looking at her, still screaming, the professor calls out, "If you leave early it counts as an absence." Katherine growls something inaudible and pushes through the door, leaving the noise and eyes behind her as it shuts, muffled in the closed classroom, but still shouting and burning.

chapter 4

cold quiet in the med center waiting room. Cough cough, distant beeping, low murmur of a TV turned down to almost-nothing, spitting out news, CNN ticker-tape like an unspooled hypnotist's spiral. Katherine slumps in the uncomfortable chair, presses further into the picky yellow fabric, Kevin Killian's *Argento Series* open in her lap. Only a few other bodies pepper the waiting room, breathe warm air into the sterile cold.

Katherine was still trying to stop her body from shaking, unable to drive the memory of her trip here from her mind, the vivid recollection of her voice escaping her lips but not hers, words she would never use, a tone she felt no emotional connection with. The teens leaning on their car looking up at her. At first thinking she was on some kind of joke until she flashed middle fingers and repeated her insults. Repeated these bold claims she couldn't stop herself from letting slip. Her eyes were the only things that betrayed her disconnect from mind to communication, and when the teens approached, understandably upset, the eyes lead them to think this poor girl mad. High on something. Somehow broken. They turned away and before Katherine could let loose another string of chaos she ran as fast as she could away from the two young men.

A flashing commercial on the TV catches her drifting attention, the gone eyes of the children selling toys and sweets, the bright flashes of color, logos, the false smiles of adults staring down plastic food. The light flickers, almost pours from the screen. It *does* pour from the screen, splashing slow-motion like the blood-elevator in *The Shining*, washing the waiting room in electric colors, rainbow hues of paint dripping and coating the scuffed white floor, the faded yellow of the nearby chairs. It froths a little as it hits the ground, like a multi-colored wave, rushes up against an old man staring into space, enveloping his features in smooth liquid. It engulfs a young boy, 8 or 9, who shuffles beneath the TV on his way to the magazine rack, turning his face blue and orange with blotches of turquoise. The TV light-turned-paint didn't cease, it seemed to be coming stronger now, like sea-water entering a breach, filling the room with colorful wet, splashing closer and closer to Katherine—

"Katherine, Katherine...Houf...uh, Houy—" The nurse looks dully around the room, and back to the tablet in her hand as she tries to sound out Katherine's surname.

Katherine blinks back into awareness, blinks away the colors and splashing. "Oh, uh, that's me." She stands up and follows the nurse back into a small cubicle in a room with six or seven others just like it. The nurse doesn't say anything for a few moments as she taps frantically at the tablet in her hand.

"All right...so, what's the problem today? It says here you've been experiencing hallucinations? Correct?"

"Yes."

"Oh, that's not great, is it? How long has this been going on?"

"Uh, I've noticed it a few times over the last few weeks. They...they seem to be getting worse."

The nurse doesn't look up from the tablet. "Is this the only symptom you've been experiencing?"

"Mostly, aside from the usual, feeling tired, anxious, headaches...all the stuff I've had since I've been in school."

"I see. Any changes in lifestyle lately? Diet? New relationship? Break-up of an old one?"

"No, not really...nothing new from the past couple years."

"I see. And it says here on your paperwork, under medications recently taken, you put marijuana?"

"Uh, yeah."

"How much marijuana would you say you use, on average?"

"About a joint a day, give or take. Sometimes a little more, sometimes a little less."

"So, you use roughly every day?"

"Uh, yeah. I'll probably take a few hits every day. Occasionally I don't smoke for a day or two. So, on average."

"When was the last time you used?"

Katherine's breath caught for a second before she answered. *Used*? What the hell kind of term was that? "I mean, I took a couple hits earlier today, because I thought it might help."

The nurse's eyes narrow just a little bit, the emerald green cooling as she finally looks up from the tablet, directly into Katherine's eyes. The nurse snorts quietly, almost too soft for Katherine to hear. Almost.

"I also drank a coffee before I came here, which I put on the paperwork too, just in case you needed to know about it."

"Uh-hm. So, look, you are having an adverse reaction to a powerful narcotic. You will be fine, but for now, you need to just calm down."

Katherine is stunned. The small room wavers in and out of focus, highlighted options, fight or flight, waiting for player two into infinity, waiting for you to put in another quarter, waiting to press continue—

Fight it is. Katherine's too tired to keep running. "Look, lady, this has nothing to do with smoking pot, something is really wrong with me! Don't give me this reefer madness horseshit, help me figure out what is going on!"

"Whoa, easy now. I told you what is going on, you need to calm down. If you can't calm down, I'll have to call the police. You've been using too much of an illegal, schedule 1 drug, which can have any number of severe side effects, including auditory and visual hallucinations—"

Katherine growls, low, guttural, a sound she never knew she was capable of making. The nurse looks at her coldly. Katherine turns and leaves the small room. The nurse watches her go but doesn't try to follow. They already ran her credit card, so let her go.

Bring on the drinking. Bring on the smoking. Bring on the whatever pills we can get from Joey. Katherine's life like a montage, of liquor store runs, picking up bags from dealer's houses, plumes of smoke and piles of empty bottles. The way the light reflects off them. Bent cigarettes from crushed soft-packs. Her walks becoming obstacle courses of temptations and pit-falls, avoid the dangers, avoid the street and the cars in it. Avoid punching the beefcake in front of you in the back of the head for no reason. Avoid open manhole covers and lopsided steps. Avoid looking at anyone or anything for too long. Avoid any kind of open bottle of cleaner or chemicals.

As she is walking in the door of her apartment, Katherine feels a strange shifting in her mouth, a looseness in her gums. She walks into the bathroom and looks in the mirror. A number of teeth in her upper jaw are darkening. Faint lines of cracks begin snaking across them. One falls out directly, without Katherine even touching it. She lets out a startled whimper as she presses one of the other teeth, seeing it tip to the side as she applies the light pressure. She winces, and pulls the tooth from her mouth with barely any force at all. A blink, and everything is back the way it should be, all the rot gone, the lost pieces of her body returned.

chapter 5

had only actually been inside Joey's house once or twice, during the day. Now, at night, you could see the money in every light-reflecting surface and soft lamp fixture. In every piece of crystal or marble around the two floors. Antique wood tables. Every painting hung almost nonchalantly on hall walls, in the entry-way, a real Rothko in the first-floor bathroom. Katherine is more used to her mother's second-hand furniture, old couch she's had since Katherine was in high school, the one they got from her grandma when she moved into an assisted-living home. Worn beds passed down from cousins or tenuous family friends. Her own Ikea chair, bought used and deeply discounted on Craigslist, only a little bit of a funny smell. But here, these were things people never used. There were whole rooms people seemed to hardly traverse. Uncracked tombs. Immaculate carpeting. Leather sofas without a crease or indent at all. There is a bar on the first floor, and a bar downstairs. Nearly all of the bottles stocked in the downstairs one are full and have unbroken caps.

Drinks all around. Katherine doesn't say much as the group finds their place among the expensive furniture and Joey's big mouth. Bragging about the house, about the wood coffee table imported from Brazil, about the amount of money invested in the back yard. Bragging about the price of the booze. Katherine notices it doesn't taste quite as good after she finds out how stupidly expensive it is.

"C'mon, guys, let's play a game or something. We can't just stand around getting drunk, we need to do *something*," E says impatiently. Katherine is glad she isn't the only one bored by Joey's boasting.

"Drinking games with *this* liquor? No way. It's way too expensive to just waste on that," Joey says matter-of-factly.

"Well what the hell do you expect us to do all night?" Landry asks, examining one of the sculptures in the living room. It has eyes and a strange grin, and for a moment Katherine almost thinks it is another hallucination.

"I have a better idea. Who's up for a little hot-tubbing?" Joey smiles his pervy smile at this, looks a bit too long at Katherine. The group look between each other skeptically. No one moves or says anything. "Fine. How about we just go check out the old arcade games in the guest house?"

Place like a dream. Old arcade cabinets, 80s, 90s. Flicker of neon, Katherine closes her eyes against the greens and reds and bitter oranges, train wreck in the back of her head building, creeping up the base of her neck and back of her throat. There is silence, briefly, Joey stops talking. Katherine opens her eyes. Around the room are a soda machine. Popcorn maker. Old gas station signs on the tall walls like chain restaurant fake-homeliness. There are faces shuffling around the carpeted room. Black moth at corners of her eyes. Reaching for the movement, finding only dead space. No one appears to notice.

"This is vintage, first generation Pac-Man, from Japan. We had it reprogrammed to be in English." Joey again filling the air with noise. Jolt of something like fear in her breathing, heavy and grating, weighing every breath. Katherine worried the others will hear the ragged intake of air. Sediment embedded in her lungs.

"This whiskey tastes cheap," Katherine growls, though it doesn't. Her brain screams It Doesn't! but her mouth doesn't try to relay the message.

"Fuck you! That is 120-dollar whiskey! You can't tell the difference because you've never been able to afford something this expensive in your life!"

"Hey, Joey—" E begins.

"What, she started it! 'This whiskey tastes cheap'...don't come in my home and insult the liquor I give you, FOR FUCKING FREE! That's not fucking cool!"

Katherine wants to apologize. Actually wants to say sorry to the whiny little shit. Instead, she simply raises the crystal glass in her hand, upturns it, emptying its contents onto the immaculate white carpet, and lobs the crystal through the monitor of the Pac-Man cabinet, shattering the glass and sending sparks and dying-glitches of 8-bit music into the air.

Everyone, including Katherine, screams, voices raise into one indignant note between them, Joey's face collapses open, eyes near tears, staring at the jagged hole punched in the now darkened screen.

Katherine doesn't hear them anymore as she turns and leaves, doesn't feel herself brush off Landry's panicked hands on her shoulder, doesn't comprehend herself stepping out of the house and into the cold night air, onto the street, breath ragged slurping in the darkness, coat and purse somewhere back inside, somewhere back of memory. Feet moving on their own. Eyes blank, dissolved. Mind blank, dissolving, finding unbuttoned fabric and red mashed fruit before the slate—

Back in her apartment, Katherine has begun to feel more normal. Heart rate slowing back down, wavy vision settling into familiarity, her stomach not trying to leap out her throat anymore. She is smoking a cigarette, and watching lions prowl their territory on the television. Lions stretch and roar. Katherine can't seem to take her eyes from the screen. Lions stalk, they leap, they shout. She can feel their rhythm, the rise and fall of their breathing, the smell of the rotten meat on their breath. She can almost feel their rough tongue on her hands, feel the pierce of teeth on the soft skin between her thumb and forefinger. Sharp pain. Real pain.

Katherine looks down and realizes she has been pressing the small pair of scissors from the table in front of her into her hand. She drops them, alarmed, and watches the single, thick droplet of blood push out from the wound and run down the side of her hand and arm. She takes another slug of whiskey and a hit off her cigarette, trembling.

Mesmerized by the long slow movements of the bread slicer. Running loaves through the clanking metal blades. *A disturbed music all the way to the moon and stars.* Katherine hears lullabies and familiar melodies. Sees an intriguing light between the blades. Shimmer of holographic foil, maybe it's a Pokémon card or an arcade token stuck between the shaking metal. Calling, calling. I think my childhood might be somewhere in there, behind those blades. *I'm restless to put my fist through that pit stop—*

A short blond woman steps out into the bakery, buttoning her chef's coat. She washes her hands slowly, deliberately, and Katherine waits to acknowledge her until she is done.

"Hey, Louise."

"Hello. How has it been today?" The woman looks around the department wearily, eyeing the display tables with a small frown.

"Busy, but not the worst. How are you?" Katherine asks, trying to sound genuinely interested.

"I'm good. Listen, Katherine, can we talk for a minute?"

In Louise's office, a small concrete bunker behind the seafood department that perpetually smells like shrimp and burning onions, Louise looks at Katherine, solemnly.

"So, Katherine, I'm going to cut right to the chase here. You've received a customer complaint, about, uh, you...she said you were—" Louise looks down at a piece of paper in front of her, "—'rude to her' on Tuesday the 15th at the bakery counter. She said you 'just walked away' from her while she was talking to you?"

"Ok, hold on, Louise, first of all, *she* was being rude, and I just—"

"Look, Katherine, you know how important our reputation is with our customers. And part of that is that our customer service is flawless. People come in with expectations of what our customer service will be, and we want to 'Wow' them. Go beyond that expectation. It's one of our biggest draws, as a store. So, if that customer service isn't up to the All Foods standard, you know..."

Louise's voice begins trailing off, but her mouth is still moving. Sounds—strange voices, not hers, organ music warbling, the grinding of metal—all begin to come from it. Quietly at first, rising in volume, as Louise continues miming talking, the sound in the room echoing off the bare white walls. Katherine nods as if she is following, tries to block out the drone of the noises, unsuccessfully, feeling an anxiety welling in her at the over-stimulation, this cannot continue this way—

"Do you understand?" Louise asks, a normal voice, all other noises gone. Katherine blinks once, and nods unsteadily.

"Ok, good. You can do it, I know you can, you just have to try a little harder. You have to put in the effort to get the benefits. Thanks, Katherine."

chapter 6

people noises everywhere. Sea of faces, of blue and salmon-colored jerseys, hats, whipping-towels. Sea of face paint and screaming, of dogs and cheese sauce. The sky is blue and immense above the open stadium. On the field, the players zip and fleck, little dots among the white lines and green lawn-waves. Katherine nurses a coke unsteadily, watching the way the clouds roll across the stadium and leave giant shadow-footprints as they pass over it, not particularly interested in football. Landry sits next to Katherine, squinting down through the sun at the minuscule players popping around the field. Katherine gives up any attempt to pretend she is following the game, and begin marveling at the strange crowd around her. Dizzying crowd.

Echoing voices like hard edges. Pointy corners. Bonking shins and poking soft flesh. Is she bruising from sound? Like firecrackers, movement to all sides, explosions of motion at the corners of her eyes. A wave washes across the crowd and it takes Katherine a moment to realize it isn't just a trick of her eyes. The motion makes her more dizzy, unable to take her eyes from it as it works around the stadium again. Noise like body blows or some intrusive scent. Get it away from me—Get away! Katherine feels her heart beating too fast, feels a monstrous dilation of the pores, from which sinuous flayings of tissues under the teguments appear, wriggling, living mass not of her own body—

Katherine leaps up, and Landry looks at her with concern. Katherine mumbles something about using the bathroom, she picks her way unsteadily through the wavering crowd, still assaulted by the sound, juttering movements all around her, feeling slithering things beneath her skin.

As she rushes up the steps toward the exit, it is as if each face she passes is turning and shouting at her. Some voices she can understand, others she can't. "We used to have a friendship!" "What are you kicking about?" "You didn't tell me! About him, or any of it!" "Hot Diggity Dog!" "A Monstrous hybrid of human and animal." "But I can't go without you—" "Try and describe this creature! See who listens!" "Come now, young lady, you're not ill! You're just exhausted!" "You did everything WRONG!" so many voices as she tries not to hear them, tries to keep the dizziness and swaying at bay, tries not to *fall...*

The faces aren't faces anymore outside the stadium, just swirls of inkblots, gnashing teeth and flesh-stumps. Shapes of human-like meat dripping and bobbing and slobbering at her.

Get home. She tells herself. *Just get home.*

Eyes teeming with maggots and fluids, with the stark light of dreams. Something crawls across her forehead in the mirror, a thin wriggling shape, and pierces the surface just above her right eye, poking out through the pink opening, no blood, just rain-slicked sides and little white foamy bits. A movement under the skin, bird smell, a snake head wriggling between her eyebrows, and it suddenly squirms back under the skin. Vibrating rebar tension. Katherine's eyes well up with tears, her stomach lurches against the paunch of her bellyskin. Her right hand twitches, meat minced and dancing, she barely stifles a wet low moan. What parts of this are real and what parts aren't? Signs refuse to say anymore.

In her apartment, she feels a little less afraid. She feels faintly safe. In her apartment, smoking and scrolling webpages. Find some symptoms similar to hers. The things not there being there. The parts of her body which seem to falter or crumble. Change. The hallucinations. The voices. A bit of searching and she finds a promising result, a site with the title "These 5 symptoms could mean danger!" Should she click this link? Open this door? She can't help think of the time she called her mom sobbing because she found out—through her various searching online, mind you—she had eclampsia. She checked off the symptoms for her mother, who told her everything sounded right, except for the fact that to have eclampsia, she would have to be pregnant. Katherine went quiet.

"You aren't..."

"No, Mom, God. I guess I missed that in the lists of symptoms I found."

So, Katherine is weary about attempting to diagnose herself online. At least this is someplace to start. *Just don't let it get to you.*

Anxious over the screaming body. Anxious in every room she enters. Are the pieces in order? Is there anything to laugh at her about? Does she look like the collection of human features she is supposed to be? Find the fault, find the places her body fails her.

These are the pieces which I predict failing:

First the lungs. Asthma-ridden, sucking dumbly oxygen, never enough.

Pulse of broken breath, shudder of the sacks in my chest. Coated with slick blackness from smoking. Even if we give it all up right now, nowhere for the residue to go. Carry tarpits in plastic bags.

Next the eyes. Already having more trouble reading things, already feeling the strain on the backs of the eyeballs, the sides of the eyeholes, from squinting. Feeling the tired muscles at the back of my nose.

I read a story online about a man who became septic after he bit a stray hangnail from one of his fingers and almost died. This was never an option until then.

Too many years of sucking in my gut. Holding it enough that I have to think about it to let it out now. Constant taught muscles. My stomach will probably just up and collapse one day. Give up, spill outwards, shrivel and flop.

Teeth...We've already been there. Move along.

Neck and back won't be long. Always waking up stiff, always sore. Straining them more. Sharp ripples of tension move through them throughout the day, beginning in one shoulder, finding the path up through the neck, the head, sometimes leaving a pulsing migraine as it passes, finally ending up in the other shoulder to settle. Sometimes, it makes that circuit in reverse again.

My mind. Like my mothers, slow meltdown. Firecracker reactor disaster, this land won't be inhabitable forever. Flash it while you can, breath the fresh air while it still licks the back of your brain. Fill every little nook and cranny now so the fire will take longer to burn out. Give it enough to chew on for a while, squeeze the last little drops from it—

chapter 7

loud bar, talking over talking over talking. Voices in semi-darkness, wash of low-lights, colors the soft lamp glows. Shimmer off the bottle of beer that sits sweating in front of Katherine. Her head swims, eyes low and heavy, lids like curtain calls. Next to her sits a cute boy, an engineering student, talking to her about one of his classes, but she is just staring into his hazel eyes, missing his words, watching the way his face and mouth moves as he speaks. Rihanna comes on over the speakers.

"Do you want to dance?"

The cute boy stops his mouth moving mid-word, face unreadable in the shadows of the bar, hair electric tips from the red light on the wall behind him. Katherine stands and reaches shakily toward him.

"C'mon."

Landry is sitting across the table facing her own cute boy-thing, and watches Katherine with mild concern.

"Ok...," the boy toy replies slowly.

"Let's go, stop being a fuckwad!"

Katherine nearly drags him behind her, and Landry stands up.

"Do you want to?" Landry asks her date. He shrugs.

"Sure. Your friend's kinda buzzed, isn't she?"

Landry nods and gives a small smile. They make their way toward the dance floor, packed with writhing limbs and bodies, soft strobing of lights. Landry steals a glance at her phone in the darkness, seeing the long text she had sent Katherine a couple nights prior, about cooling it on the drinking, both of them, though Landry had really only meant Kat. She saw Katherine's face flash through a beam of blue light, dark and a bit scary-looking, yelling something indecipherable in the crowd. At least she looked happy tonight...

The four figures press and stumble their way to the bar's exit, a large stairwell filled with harsh orange halogen light, almost painful compared to the throb of colors they had just left behind. The building is five stories, each floor a different theme, and the four figures are on the highest level. Katherine sways even more heavily, leaning into the cute boy with the hazel eyes and murmur words that go straight by Katherine's head. Landry is the first to creep to the barrier at the edge of the stairwell, a small wall about six inches wide and four feet high. She peers down the wide spiral, five floors. Katherine and the two boys join her with their noses just over the edge, looking into the open space below.

"Kat went to school with that kid who fell down there a couple years ago...what was his name?" Landry says, a tinge of grotesque excitement in her voice.

"Yeah, I, like, had classes with him and everything. I went over and swam in his pool once when we were kids. I used to buy weed from him, too, in high school, sometimes."

"Holy shit, that's crazy, dude." Landry's boy honks stupidly, and Landry consoles herself that he is still incredibly pleasant to look at, at least.

"I remember hearing about that shit on the news," Katherine's boy adds, letting go of Katherine to lean over the wall just a little, thinking about the way a body would cut through the empty space, the way it might flail, the way *he* might flail, as he fell.

Katherine looks suddenly vacant, but the other three are too preoccupied with the thought of dropping the five stories straight down to notice her. She steps slowly away from the group, along the barrier edge. In one quick motion she pulls herself up onto the ledge and stands straight up, swaying slightly, eyes never blinking or focusing on anything in particular. She begins to walk along the ledge, imitating a tight-rope walker, swaying, eyes still gone, face straight ahead in a lost look of confusion or nothing at all. Landry looks up first, and lets out a low moan, gasping mixed with barking. The two boys look up in unison at Landry's strangled yelp.

"Holy shit!"

"Whoa, cool!"

"Katherine! What the fuck are you doing?! Get down right now!"

Katherine continues, not acknowledging the trio at her feet. She passes them, growing a bit more unsteady, and just before the half-way point, she slips and begins teetering. Body wavers, shimmy from side to side, try to regain balance. Try to regain control. Can't. Katherine topples forward, her body pitching off the ledge, toward the hole in space, toward the abyss. Landry's boy manages to get an arm around her leg as she goes, holds tight, too much off-balance to do anything but hold her dangling over the pit. Katherine's eyes suddenly pop back to life. Like a TV screen flickering on, eyes wake then go wide, terror rips across her face, the screaming starts, hers, Landry's, she begins struggling without realizing it, without controlling it, and as the second boy gets a hand on her both young men have trouble keeping a grip. As Landry pulls with them, Katherine's terrified frame finally peeks back over the barrier. One final heave and the four of them are a pile on the floor, panting, Landry and Katherine weeping, both boys in shock, drawing heavy breaths. The door opens and two young men with their collars popped, wearing Ed Hardy shirts and large sunglasses step into the stairwell. They see the people on the ground, some weeping, some muttering expletives under their breath, and turn back into the bar, shaking their heads.

Katherine wants to remember the entire trip home, as vividly as her drunken state will allow her. To make up for that lapse; one minute cuddling up next to her date, she can't even remember his name anymore, thinking about how dirty her apartment was, wondering if he seemed non-creepish enough to suggest finding their way back to his, when suddenly she's being pulled back from the top of the stairwell at the bar, that same spot where that kid fell when we were in high school. Capturing the lights as they raced across the car's windshield, the glow of the Marriott building, purple and electric, the cartoons or plastic toys of her childhood. Watching the puffs of breath of people on the sidewalks and emerging from parking structures, from building fronts, almost like little comic book word bubbles, she thinks she can read what they are saying, or thinking.

At some point after getting her home, Landry tells Katherine that she is worried about her, that she needs to get some help. Landry tells her she is going to set up an appointment for her with her own therapist.

Katherine is upset at this, but mostly just because we feel we should be. Can't seem to bring ourselves to care one way or the other, honestly. Time is jittery and we can't get a hold of it. Landry voice comes like an after-thought, an old text coming back. It sounds like it is from another room, another space in time. Katherine hears the words Landry says but feels as if they are already written in her past.

As Landry closes the door, Katherine sees movement above her bed, all the 5 X 9 photographs she had tacked there, the mix of black & white shots and color, of friends and famous people, of art of her own creation and the creation of others, all were moving. Dancing, swaying, walking briskly across and out of the frame. The light blinks off, and Katherine sees each face turn toward her, eyes glowing eerily, smiles stretching in unison, some sinister echo across the photographs. Katherine pulls the blanket over her head and shuts her eyes as tightly as she can. *Maybe Landry was right...maybe I do need help...*

chapter 8

isn't like a therapist's office. At least, not the ones she's seen in movies and on TV. There is no sexy black leather, no wood grain, no expensive vaguely modernist sculptures, no fancy TV or fish tank. It looks more like the guidance counselor's office from high school. A bit dull, cold. But clean. The secretary taps away at her computer, quiet, unassuming. One other person, a thin man in his late forties, sits in the waiting room with Katherine, his wet red eyes looking at the grey-green carpeting. Katherine skims a copy of Kathy Acker's *Blood and Guts in Highschool* as she sits, not really taking any of the words in. She can't stop fidgeting, first her feet, then legs, bouncing upwards, skittering sideways. Fingers and hands are next, dancing and trembling all on their own. Palms, wrists, up through her knees, her hips sway and shake, shoulder blades pop to unheard music. The man in the waiting room doesn't seem to notice, or at least is ignoring Katherine. The secretary takes a clipboard of papers around the corner and away. Katherine's heart races, her body seems to be standing itself up on its own, making for the exit door. Katherine wants to call out but cannot, her voice held back by stiff muscles and frozen vocal cords. Hand on the doorknob, a flash of feeling, of the cold metal against palm-flesh, then nothing as she pushes her way out the door and into the lobby. Her eyes scream to the door man as she passes, but her smile and the slight shake her hips and ass produce cause him to only smile and nod and stare as she walks quickly past. Perception, thought falter. World is turning black and the body still presses forward. We are not in control of this mechanism—

"So, how'd it go?" Landry sits straight-backed across from Katherine in one of the little pizzeria's booths. Pops and pizza spread out before them.

"Good...really good. I like him. He seems..."

"Yeah, like a good doctor, right? I mean, he isn't one of those ones who play the stupid games or tried to hypnotize me or anything. And he doesn't seem like a creep, so I guess that's a plus."

"Uh-huh, he seems, more professional, definitely." Katherine pokes at the pizza on the plate before her, pushing puddles of cheese and sauce from her slice. What could she even say to Lan? Where would she even start?

"Well, I'm glad. You'll be surprised how much he can help you, when you look back on it. I mean, look at my parents. We thought for sure they'd get divorced before I got into high school, and look at 'em now." Landry smiles a tight smile, and Katherine returns it. "When are you going back?"

"Oh, we scheduled another appointment for...next week." Katherine steadies her face. She had never been very good at lying, to anyone, but especially not people that knew her. Bad poker-face. Landry reads the creases and muscles of Katherine's features, and seems satisfied with this answer.

"Great. Did you hear about the thing with Joey?"

Her mind speeds, fingers flick buttons without thinking, first fb, check email, log-in to school email just in case anything didn't forward. Then back to fb, skim a couple stories from people she can hardly recall from high school, mind is straight-flat plain, drifting line without peaks, mind doesn't grasp the things flashing by. Check WebMD, then finally Wiki. What to search? Katherine has been stuck in her research, unable to find any clues from what few leads she has stumbled across. She begins typing, and sees the word appear in the text box before it materializes in her brain. She begins with 'hallucinations' and moves on from there, spinning the little wheel on the mouse and clicking softly in the darkness. Webs of connections, continuations, dead ends and weird gutters. A chill-hop station blends the old with the new on the television, thumping melodies out of time, mixing with the room's warm stale air. How many links how many rabbit holes how many windows jimmied and popped out? How many dead-end pop ups and pages and broken links? False leads. She floats, floats, pulls herself along the rocks and the algae, searches the wash, the breaking waves, drags her hands through the sand and silt, keep looking. Answers are there, find them. Find them hiding. A rough spot in the current, a pointy edge buried in the mud. A name. Rawling. Find it again. Rawling. This name knows something.

That was that same name, from before. Rawling. Who the fuck is this guy? Click click. Time softly chitters away on electric lines, 1s and 0s, counted in load times and low humming. Katherine begins digging. Buried on such and such date. Such and such years old. Doctorate from generic public-Ivy league University. OK, but in what? What the hell did he do? And why did he write an essay on hallucinations *and* the predatory habits of cats? Why was she finding weird little whispers about him on the corners and gross shower drains of the internet?

As soon as she finds one story praising Dr. Rawling's research she finds another condemning it as quackery; as liberal propaganda; as conservative propaganda; as a Chinese hoax; as a US hoax to trick China; as just plain incorrect. So many sides, so many voices . . . are any true?

Finding the word *toxoplasmosis* over and over...a parasite contracted from cat feces. Can cause altered behavior, strange thinking, sometimes hallucinations.

Jesus.

Katherine keeps reading. So many things about this fly red flags for her. All of it seems too familiar, almost to the point of taking her breath away. *This is it, it has to be...all the symptoms are there...*

A quick search and Katherine finds parasite specialists in the city to be incredibly expensive. No surprise. She eyes the bill for the med-center visit next to her computer. *It's keep digging, then, I guess...*

Katherine falls asleep watching a video of Dr. Ross lecture in a stiff monotone on the metabolism of the parasites, and for once she doesn't dream, just floats in darkness.

"So, what next? I brought *Hellraiser*, *The Fly*, and both *Ginger Snaps*. I mean, the good two, at least. Any thoughts?" Katherine smiles, holding the stack of DVDs in front of her. Terry has a sudden warm memory of Kat, sitting in nearly the same spot, holding a stack of movies they'd rented from the video store, smiling the same warm, giddy smile, flashing blue eyes. Where'd that smile go? Where'd it been hiding? Terry hadn't seen it in some time, lost in a series of hard lines and shadows and coldness. Fake little smirks, almost just a twitch of corners of her mouth and nothing else, they were so faint. It made her happy to see her daughter's face like this again. Even if it was only briefly.

"Oh, I don't care, kiddo. I'd say either *The Fly*, or *Ginger Snaps*. The first one. But you pick. Anything is fine with me." Terry smiles broadly and pats her daughter's arm.

"Ok, I'm gonna grab some more chips, you want anything?"

"Oh, grab me one of those...y'know..." Terry looks toward the kitchen to try to help visualize the word she is looking for.

"A Pepsi?"

"No, y'know, the...um...food, the uh, frozen..."

"—Fudgsicle. Got it. Coming right up."

Something is waiting for her in the kitchen. Hurt and angry and glimmering in the near-darkness. She can feel it. Recognizing the scent of lavender in the shadows, and dried flesh. Black bugs shrieking, eggshell vomit noises, hiss of bubbling pale green fluid across the dirty linoleum, dragon eyes in the background music.

Katherine enters the brightly lit kitchen to find it empty. She shivers just a little as she checks the corners, all the areas something could be hiding and even those in which nothing could be.

As she enters the living room, Katherine's chest constricts, and she is unable to let escape the gasp growing in her throat and stomach. Behind her mother stands some *thing*...It's as if Katherine's eyes can't even stand to see it, it flickers and wavers, is there and then isn't, some choppy piece of film or rapid blinking. The thing stands silent, not sobbing but grinning, laughing. Dragging its dirty fingernails across its own soft chest, blackened blood, hair and rotten skin in clumps. Her mother still transfixed by the film on the television, cold sweat covering Katherine's entire body, her face feeling flushed, small blue petals withering into themselves, vibrating in her lower ribs, the creature still gibbering without sound in the corner of the room. Katherine makes herself move, makes her calves flex and lift, her knees pulling tendons, upward, makes motion, forcing herself to walk toward the creature, to not collapse, to not begin screaming. Her mother still doesn't seem to notice anything, smiling at Katherine as she returns to her spot on the couch. Cold breathing from the corner of the room. How long can she pretend it isn't there? It shuffles a little, creeps a little closer to her. Katherine feels the thundering of her pulse, the moisture beneath her arms, on the small of her back. Her eyes turn back to the television set. A girl tries to chop her tail off in the bathtub. Katherine tries to hold focus but just keeps getting blurry. That thing is still hovering at the corner of her vision, still smiling ghoulishly at her. Bared rotten teeth and dripping saliva. Her mother enraptured in the film, can't see or hasn't seen the creature yet. The blemish in the room. The tumorous spirit hovering and rolling like sticky fog, always keeping just on the edge of Katherine's periphery. It laughs again, a sick wet little sound, grinding cigarette butts in bus seats, the sound of slurping blood from a single pore like a hemoglobic milkshake. Katherine shivers, tries to focus on the girl who is becoming a creature on the screen, the girl with the growing bloodlust, the girl with the sharp new fangs, the power of new found sexuality, the craving to rip flesh and fumble in the backseat of cars—

The thing behind her mother's chair moves with incredible speed, suddenly rushing toward Katherine, a trail of dark mist streaming behind it. Katherine screams and jumps up as it nears her, and she closes her eyes involuntarily, still screaming. For a long moment she feels nothing in the darkness, and then feels a warm touch. Hears her mother's voice.

"It's all right...it's all right...c'mon, shh, are you okay honey?" Katherine opens her eyes to her mother's soft voice, and presses herself further into the hug.

"I'm...I'm sorry...I must have dozed for a second and..." She trails off and lays her head on her mother's shoulder, her breathing slowing, her heartbeat a thick shuddering in her own chest, vibrating against her mother's. The older woman stays silent, smiles comfortingly at Katherine. Katherine gives up trying to hold back tears, and lets them fall, quiet and cool and salty, down her face and onto her mother's old pink sweater.

chapter 9

seat of sensations. That bakery at night, nearly closing. Left-over lingerings of scent, the last waft of baked bread, the cookies, the over-oiled croutons—just stale pan loaves run through the slicer sideways and lathered in Italian seasoning. Katherine feels her energy slipping away with the sunlight outside the large glass windows looking onto the parking lot. Preparatory pleasure, knowing this night is almost over. Past the half-way point, the crowds would begin to thin. The rude and privileged replaced by the drunk, the down-on-their-luck, but usually the more civil. Katherine would take the poor customer over the wealthy any day. They usually said please and thank you, and understood how a queue worked.

Mary, one of the older women who worked nights one or two days a week, is helping a customer near the bagels, and the tone of irritation in her voice draws Katherine back from the sunset and her spacing.

"—Well, look, like I said, this is just how they are. With these ones, they're more sugary, so they get a little darker on the bottom. It's a caramelization thing. It's just how they are." Mary is always curt and she often sounds irritated in normal conversation, but Katherine can tell when frustration actually sets in.

"I have been a patron of this establishment for a long time, and I have never seen them this burnt. I mean, these are *burnt*. Not caramelized, not browned. Burnt."

"Well, look, I don't know what to tell you. That's all we have today. I mean, you don't have to buy it, if you don't want."

Katherine leaves the two of them and heads into the back room to find a rack for the left-over cookies and bars. Mary follows her a few moments later.

"Can you frickin' believe this woman?! I mean, my God, I'm not racist, but this is the kind of person that makes me almost use the 'n' word. God, just *rude*." Mary flies past Katherine, who slowly pushes the rack out front, feeling numb. *What the fuck?! What the fuck do I say to that?!* Nothing. She'd said nothing, and knew, even as much as she wanted to, even if she thought of some perfect response, and found the perfect moment, she'd say nothing. The way her gut vibrated and her bowels clenched and all the hairs on her arms and neck began to sit up, she knew she was too afraid of conflict to say anything. To call out this woman. *Racist-ass old bitch.*

Tension only she feels. Tension tasting of old blood and bad apples. Of genocide and white paint on everything. Tension a waft of sour meat, the trash-can's residual summer smell, some barbecue while a human body sways from a fraying rope, the sound of honky-tonk shit-kicking drowning out screams and blues moans. Sudden shifting, tension pressing against the levy, the sides bulge, rivets exploding outward from the strain, tension spraying in little streamers of water through the bolt-holes, the entire thing shakes and vibrates—

"The fuck is wrong with you?" Mary stops dead in her tracks. Katherine feels her face go flush. Why had she said that? She was thinking it, sure, but she hadn't wanted to actually *confront* Mary...had she? The woman looks at Katherine for a moment, a cold look on her face.

"Me?" Mary growls, finally. "What the hell is *your* problem? Don't tell me you are on her side!"

"I'm on the side of not being a fucking racist, you old bag!" Katherine spits back. Where did that come from? She tries to make her mouth stop, tries to will the air and vibration welling-up from her diaphragm, the cords tensing and shaking in specific tones to halt, but she can't. "I'm on the side of treating people like human beings."

Mary just stares at Katherine. She steps toward her, Katherine feels a fight brewing and cannot seem to stop herself from readying for it. Mary pulls her jacket off and throws it at Katherine.

"Screw this. I don't need people insulting me like this, calling me frickin' racist! I have a ton of black friends, ok?! You don't even know me! I'm outta here. Have fun closing by yourself tonight." She storms out of the bakery, leaving Katherine reeling but regaining control of her extremities, though her mouth still doesn't seem to be working. She watches Mary step briskly out of the store before calling Louise to tell her what happened.

Lying on her back, blowing smoke rings toward the grainy ceiling, Katherine thinks about Bubba the cat. About all the times she got caught smoking in the high school parking lot. About *The Magic School Bus*, about her first concert, about the way that last boyfriend, Elliott, would leave his dirty cups all around the apartment. About the first time she came, home alone and watching a Jewel music video on TV. About anything but this thing that might be inside her, might just be her. She thinks about her hair—

Always self-conscious about it. All through elementary school, middle school, even into high school, to save money her mother would cut her hair. And it was *fine*...she did as good a job as she could, but...No one really said anything explicitly, but it was always there. Unspoken. Like a joke whispered around her, avoiding her, the other girls laughing quietly when her back was to them. That is why she hadn't had it cut in sometime, dreaded somewhat the thought of losing the helmet protecting her head and her shame, her padding between her off-kilter mind and the world.

Fray of static. Pulling, pulling. Katherine's hands grip little locks of her hair. That urge to keep tugging, like biting a hangnail off that you know will bring a chunk of skin with it, like that too-hot bathwater you can't help but keep pressing into, pinkish flesh and all. Like walking smiling into the headlights of oncoming traffic. Slit your throat in an alley full of felines—

Huh?!—

pulling, pulling, that hair-strand never ending, growing thicker in her grip, growing more frizzy and scratchy. Worms twisted, oily tentacles, strands of her own bad hair. Pulling thread from the soft spot on top of her head, wrapping like twine, pulling from all corners and sides of her scalp, drawing into the single thread like water into a napkin, thickening. Katherine's hands keep unraveling, keep twirling without her. She tries to stop them but just feels the hair ripping from the little holes it shoots from, strand by strand. Thicker and heavier. Katherine looks down at the pile before her and realizes her hair has become something synthetic. Something fake. Doll hair or old hemp rope, still streaming from the top of her head like she is spurting it. She feels nauseous. She closes her eyes, tries to tune out the movement, the sights, but still hears the fake strands popping out of her scalp, still feels the thick and fuzzy and wrong locks in her hands. She tries to scream, only spits little mouthfuls of tangled Barbie hair. Can't breathe, can't stop

pulling—

Everything is gone when Katherine opens her eyes again. Her hair normal feeling, in the place it should be, the strange pile covering her legs gone, her mouth free and clear of twirling wads. She looks around, unsure what to do. She simply collapses, to the floor, dazed.

How to keep from screaming? Name all the different kinds of dinosaurs you can, one by one. Dance with your favorite. Kiss the tips of your fingers. Stay away from New York City. Chronicle all occurrences. Find yourself on a drive, split the difference of your sandwich with a chipmunk. Know your family history. Know when you're not alone. Find the beginnings of inhibitions and snuff them out. Or ramp them up. Distract. Distract.

How much more of this can she take? Every part of her anatomy tingles with soreness, with exhaustion. She can hardly move her limbs let alone the myriad of other organs, the collection of cells, the dusting of symbiotic bacteria and critters all over her own elements. Katherine hears something scuffling next to her, and reaches down absently to pet Ricky-O as he passes.

Instead, her fingers close on the fingers of a little ice-cold hand! Rotscent, intense horror overtakes her. Nightmare, nausea, she tries to draw back her arm but the hand clings to it, and a most melancholy voice sobs—

"Who do you think runs that brain of yours?"

In grains of mirror glass grinding, in long knives 'shrrrnk-ing' together, in the sick wet plop of removed eyeballs, eyeholes with an unmistakable musk, the voice coughs—

"You are already used up, you just can't get it through your thick skull. Not yet, at least. We'll get you there. We'll carve a tunnel into it if we have, just so you finally get it, just before it's too late, we'll make you understand..."

It speaks again, almost not words, something running like current, the blood in Katherine's body, echoing in and massaging every part of her at once, vibrating and cutting.

"You speak and sing. And dread. You abstraction, you who fear dissolving flesh, and the uranium in the Earth. You think you know what fear is? I can show you that. You think you are a singular whole? Your pieces will desert you. They've already started to."

The face wavers in the darkness, shapes change, the sounds, oh god the sounds! Broken radios howling, shattered laughing turning into sobs, the final curtain call of death groans and slit throats. Metal grating of hurt on someone's mind. Inhuman fingers grab her ankle.

"It's not Miss Jessel! But at the window—bog monsters and broken dreams."

"Straight before us!" The reflection of a thousand cracked faces, a thousand opened-up bodies, organs on the outside, a thousand compounds of animals and minerals, Katherine sees the way her face shatters just as the others do—

"It's there—the coward horror, there for the last time!" Fog on her eyes, no more faces just a nightmare with no head, teeth cracking, just eyes floating, wet orbs in darkness, brackish breath coming in heaves and hisses.

Doctor whose face she can never remember when she leaves his office, hasn't seen in years. Running hands and eyes across her skin, theory of pain and the quiet acts of violence behind her eyes. Hesitant in the absence of incident. Of concrete packaged up and handed over. Something real for him to run his eyeballs over. Freckled hands, bad smell in the room.

Careful not to mention trying to harm herself, careful not to let on how close she has been to fizzling out or burning someone up with her. Trying to let the inside her loose, in any way she can. Just give him the basics, just the speakable facts, just the bits that tell him something is not right. Just enough to understand, without doing anything...drastic.

When he is done examining her, he tells her she might be suffering from some form of exhaustion, or minor mental imbalance caused by stress, by poor diet, by lack of exercise. Perhaps school is more taxing on her than she thought. Perhaps all these hallucinations, all these sick meat-slicked feelings, blood pumping across her vision, body horror manifesting itself as waking dreams along her blipping line, maybe all this was just too much essays, not enough broccoli; too much test cramming and not enough power walking, not enough Pilates, not enough fruits with the cereal in the morning. Of Course! That was it! More green veggies and it will all go away! Just stop worrying about school and it can't talk to you in a monster voice from within, it can't move you into the path of oncoming cars...why hadn't she thought of this earlier?!

"You think this is all in my head, then?" Katherine asks, feeling heat radiating from the back of her neck, around the circumference of her face.

"No—I mean, it is likely these symptoms are the result of some abnormal functioning on your part, but that doesn't mean these things don't *seem* real to you."

Katherine stares at the doctor a moment. Sees tongue depressors, scalpels, drug vials breaking the flesh of his throat like a flimsy Godzilla set. Down the esophagus. Believe me yet?!

It takes all her will to move her body up, standing, keep her hands at her sides, away from stray sharps and pre-shard glass. Float up, out, before the doctor can even form words. Out onto the street, shrouding her head against the cold rain, somewhere between water and ice, falling in thick pellets. Damp paper plane, she glides into the current of others on the sidewalk, finds the flow soothing, finds herself walking without thinking about it, finds a momentary space to press herself into and fade away.

chapter 10

alarm sounds. Sleep hasn't been for at least an hour or two now, anyway. Darkness, grogginess. Find footing. Find a way to pull herself from the warmth and softness. Find a way to pull the world back down under the covers with her. Stumble, sway, fuzzy to the bathroom, finally relieve the pain in her bladder. Slow and thick mind, a low growl, trying to shake sleep. Coffee calling, unbrewed, echoing out of the kitchen. Must begin the process. Unlatch the metal filter, knock it loudly against itself, dump as much of the old grounds as she can, never getting them all, still having to clean it out with her finger. Run it under cold water. The bag of beans in the cupboard above her head, muscles screaming for coffee stretching painfully in her back. Brain screaming for coffee. Across her shoulders, her arms. The soft tinkle of beans falling into the little black grinder, the satisfying click of the top coming down and latching. The whirl of the motor, of beans spinning, dancing, smashing into one another, collapsing into shards. The noise of the motor grows higher-pitched, more steady. Pull open the drawer, find a measuring spoon. If there isn't one, find a table spoon. Fill the metal, scoop, scoop. Somehow, she always spills a little here. Squeeze tight around the cap, it's always too tight, always feels like it's going to take more strength than she has to open it. The seal cracks, a whirring hiss. If this is the second cup a blast of steam accompanies the shriek. Unscrew the cap, put the rubber gasket back in place, it always comes off with the cap. Grasp one of the mugs from the lopsided cupboard. Feel the slick cool ceramic in her grip. Set it beneath the spout, flip the switch. And wait. Breathe slowly, blink her eyes, try to wave sleep off with will alone. But she needs help. Always does. The coffee machine screams and hisses as it works up heat and steam, starts to chug a little, a brown stream splashing down into the mug. The smell of the roasted beans, like old diners or Christmas morning. Rousing her sleep-slumped mind. The coffee machine reaches crescendo with its garbled howling, and begins to sink into silence, the last drips of liquid falling into the mug. Now the morning can begin.

Listless when she should be doing so much. Vague tiredness, vague pains in her side, in her leg, in her right forearm, hold her back. Headaches and stomachaches sap energy, nothing left for the things she should be doing. So much worry, all she seems to be able to do is sit on the couch and watch the images on the screen. Or lay in bed, immobile, encased in her blankets, a warm safe space where she hadn't felt any of the effects of whatever was going on in her brain. It was as if she had a truce with whatever was causing all this, and the bed was a neutral zone, a cease-fire quadrant in an otherwise weird and draining war.

Parasitology podcasts. Kinks and biomedicine. Such strange huddle group. Her favorite new video game. Skimming along the gutter of the internet. All disease, all sex, all curdled pie and disbelief, computer-related stuff, woman-related stuff, all wax gills and screaming. Losing time in them, hanging on the words like gold-dipped or like they might be the only thing that can save her.

When she finally takes a break from the computer, she has gathered little new information, a few tidbits about the life cycle of a number of different parasites, a young couple with similar symptoms as her own from the turn of the century, nothing especially helpful. Never a mention of Dr. Rawling and his work.

In the kitchen. Yellow lights are wet on the walls. Shiny against the little window and the last bits of sunlight filtering in. Katherine is chopping vegetables absently, slitting skins, soft limbs and extremities, roots and stalks. The cat watches her from across the room, strange look in his eye like he thinks Katherine is someone else as she pushes the scraps down the drain. She sees herself, tiny and falling after them, Alice's rabbit-hole, the garbage disposal an unending cavern, all the bits of broken food, stems and rinds, grisly and wet like a movie crime-scene. Floating downward, down, toward the whirling blades. Down, down. She cannot stop, like an inversion of the fizzy lifting room in Willy Wonka, down, down, toward the blades, we'll be chopped to ribbons! Down here we all float—

Blood and bits of muscle as she hits. Maybe that's a toe she sees flying by. Little white snowflakes of bone shards—

Katherine snaps back from her thoughts, and is herself again. As much as she can be, at least. Her own size, anyway. Her hand *is* in the disposal, though— all that blood! She feels nothing but is misted in the face with crimson droplets, delicate, warm. Chunks of flesh fly out of the hole, rubber-looking and raw and pink. She still feels nothing. A scream trapped in her throat. She pulls her arm back from the black abyss, the water gurgling frothy salmon as it drains, the disposal still running. Shrieking. Or is that her? She removes her arm, she sees her hand, still intact, clutching a blood orange, in red and pink tatters. The Moro's raw flesh looks so similar to her own it's still almost painful to see...

We have to get out of this place. It might be the last thing we ever do...

Just walk. Keep moving. The more your body works, the less the fog creeps in. The less the world goes wrong. Goes wobbly. Along the river, the wide concrete walking path, nearly alone, the grey sky humming with light just beneath, sun trapped behind smoke. Across the amphitheater and the small park, they turn into an ice-skating rink in the winter, past the museum, the old astronaut statue outside still holding itself proud and metallic. Katherine stops near the highway, the long pedestrian bridge she used to walk during high school, the one she'd had her first real kiss on. It feels like it is shimmering in and out of existence, all vibrating, all hazy half-there, solid but not, Katherine unsure if she should take another step—

All this space a body could be in. why so closed-off to the world? Why not expand into it. So many pieces, we can surely spare a few to explore the vastness. Give ourselves to the air and the sky, give ourselves to the sounds riding the wind, that could be us, who needs this old body anyways? We can become above it, move passed, we can evolve!

Katherine's feet inch closer to the edge

Go tell it on the mountain, on the water tower, go tell the city how we've found its secrets and we need to be a part of them. We need to spread our wings and turn to dust, let ourselves roll and rumble into all the crevices, all the potholes and manhole covers, etch ourselves into all the street signs—

Katherine finds herself on the edge of a tall overpass, a pedestrian bridge overlooking an alleyway. Her feet are sticking over the edge, her balance off, one false start forward and she would be toppling toward the concrete below. Heart seems to be the first to realize. Begins racing as if trying to pump itself away from danger. Then the pores. All of them, all at once. Leaking from all of them, warm terror. Then more parts follow suit, arms go heavy and rubbery, legs snap into hard beams, lungs flap to try to catch up with heart. Slowly, piece by piece, she pulls herself back from the edge. Below her a large group of cats are coming out from hiding, mangy and bone-thin all of them. Katherine hears their cries beneath her, and feels a jump in her stomach. She had been asleep, or completely out of it...she hadn't known where she was until it was almost too late...what if she had jumped or fallen off the bridge? She may have never even awoken. Another sound below brings a sudden shudder, and she looks down to see a mother stop with a baby carriage, looking at all the cats, the baby inside cooing softly. Katherine has a quick vision of what a falling body might have done to the mother and her infant, and shudders. Tears form at the corners of her eyes, her nose plugs and her throat stiffens. If she hadn't woken up when she did...

chapter II

All Foods is filled with voices echoing off the tall metal ceiling, colliding into each other on the way back down, becoming backwards-record demon sounds and gargles, unsettling soundtrack groaning and bellowing just below the level of articulating.

Trent, one of the newer team members, was helping a woman with a cake order. Katherine watches them for a moment, as Trent attempts to discern what the woman is looking for. She only nods 'yes' to the things he is saying, and he seems to be getting frazzled.

"You need some help?" Katherine asks, attempting a tone of friendship rather than authority.

Trent looks relieved. "Oh, uh...heh-heh, yeah. Thanks."

Katherine pulls the cake-book from behind the counter, and opens it in front of the woman. Trent nods as if he has just remembered this tool. The customer looks happy, and begins flipping through the pages. She points to the frosting of one, and the shape of another. Another customer has queued behind the first, with a baby strapped to her chest, shifting impatiently. The woman clears her throat exaggeratedly. Katherine hears her but pretends she doesn't.

"Excuse me," the woman finally says, looking directly at Katherine.

"We're helping this customer at the moment, but I will be with you in just a sec, thanks."

"I just can't believe it takes two of you to take one person's order."

Katherine looks up from the book, finally, glaring hard at the woman, who is smiling smugly back at her. The woman's eyes say it all: *what are you going to do about it? Say the wrong things to me, say 'em the wrong way...I'll go find your manager. I've got the power, you little peon...*

"Well, I'm still training, so Katherine here is showing me—" Trent begins, attempting to diffuse the situation. The woman simply snorts and points at one of the berries and cream cakes.

"Just one of those. One of the large ones."

The first customer looks a bit frightened, not sure what to do in the strange situation. Katherine finally takes her glare from the woman and child, and walks to the cake case. She removes the large-sized cream cake the woman pointed at, and pulls a box from beneath the counter. The woman presses past the first customer, and begins reaching for the box before Katherine has even closed it.

"Thank you. See, that wasn't so hard was it—"

Before the woman finishes, Katherine upends the cake directly onto the front of the woman, covering her with dribbling cream and streaks of blue and red from the mixed berries. The woman gasps in a choked grunt, and before she can say anything Katherine turns and walks stiffly from the bakery. She rips her jacket off and throws it at Louise, who has come running to investigate all the commotion.

"Katherine—"

"Fuck off."

chapter 12

breathe curses and spells. Feel the protection in the cigarette burns. Incantations to save the people she knows. Rituals to hold reality to the laws of her body. Write them down before this extreme point of exhaustion, of despair, of foxhole mysticism changes them. Tinges them with inversions, with absurdities. What does she look like? Godawful, to be sure. It doesn't matter. She is a husk full of long yellow faces floating like old cinematography, voices from around every corner and crease. Tearing her stomach out. Burning her nerve threads to nothing, or gnawing right through them. Who had found her lying on the apartment complex's tiny front lawn, and brought her back inside? She is sure it had happened but she can't picture it. She barely remembers how time passes. She can't feel it anymore. When was the last time she'd eaten? Her stomach in a deep squat, stretched into a rut, thin and needy. Nothing but nicotine meal and back to hiding, though. Her stomach knows enough not to complain, it is still much too dangerous around here.

A knock at the door. Katherine hears it after the first or second round, but finds the sound so unfamiliar she simply sits and continues listening to it as it grows more impatient. The muffled slap of a small fleshy ball against the cold metal slab. Katherine thinks she hears little movements of the bone and cartilage as the hand comes down onto the door. Hairs whisper faintly as they pass through the air. If Katherine looks hard enough, she can almost see the ripple of a handprint on the door in the spot the extremity is coming into contact with it. Then a familiar voice comes from the other side of the door, and signifiers suddenly meet signified in Katherine's mind. Landry! Katherine races to open the slab, and finds her friend on the other side with a barely-concealed look of worry on her face.

"Kat, you ok? You look like shit."

Katherine feels like she will break down and crumble right there in the doorway. Landry steps inside, hugging her and walking her slowly toward the couch. The tears begin, and Katherine doesn't even try to stop or hide them.

"It's OK, Kat, just start from the beginning. Tell me what's wrong."

"Look, Kat, you're not making sense, ok?" Landry looks deep into Katherine's eyes. They don't seem to be looking back. They are somewhere else. Glassed-over. "I think we should call Dr. Brundle, and maybe—"

"We can't call Dr. Brundle."

Landry's face goes cold. "What do you mean we can't call him? What happened?"

"Besides, I don't need a therapist. I need a parasitologist. I need a surgeon. I need real medical help."

"What the fuck do you mean we can't call Dr. Brundle, Katherine?" Landry's voice grows lower, a harshness draping its edges. "You have been seeing him, haven't you?"

"Look, it's just that—"

"Are you still going to him? You've been telling me you've been going."

"I tried, I just..."

"You sounded like you were trying. You, you've just been lying to me?"

"No! I mean, I went once, I just...I know it isn't going to help! Do you know how much work I've put into tracking down this information? To sift through the bullshit, the conspiracies, the smear-jobs? The false leads, the made-up symptoms...I know that *this* is what is wrong with me! This parasite—"

"Goddamnit, Kat!"

"—it causes erratic and suicidal behavior, just like—"

"You need help, and Dr. Brundle is a good psychiatrist, he can help you, if you made even a little fucking effort."

"—and hallucinations, auditory and visual. Lan, please, listen to me—"

"It's all in your fucking head, don't you get that?! There's no parasite, just your broken fucking brain!"

Katherine says nothing. Words don't form inside her head.

"You are having issues, up here, and you need someone to treat it, it's a simple as that."

"I thought you were on my side."

"Kat, there aren't any sides. I just want you to get better."

"Then listen to me! Look at the articles I found! The videos! This is the help I need! I need someone to believe me!"

Landry is silent now. Her eyes are troubling. Katherine can read the look, can almost see the thoughts passing below the thin white membrane, the sparkling blue, the small black void in the center. She could read the words "gonna call someone. Before you hurt yourself."

"Ok, Kat. I'm going to use the bathroom, and we'll look at some of the videos. I'll listen. I'm here now."

Fake words. Fake news! Fake friend. Katherine saw what she really meant, the words below the words she said. She's not going to watch the videos, listen to Dr. Rawling's evidence. She's just going to bide time until someone gets here. To take us away. Someone she's going to call. Help, she'll say. Someone to help. We don't need that kind of help. We don't need any kind. We can't let her call. If they take us, they'll watch us. We won't be able to get free. We must stop her. We must get free. That bathroom door isn't so thick. If we run at it hard enough it'll collapse for sure. Three, two, one—

The door cracks a little, and then just flies open. Landry drops her phone as she turns toward Katherine, a popping squeak erupting from her gaping mouth. Katherine, blank-eyed, rushes at her.

"Kat—"

Hands around neck. Yes, squeeze. The flesh presses back, warm and soft, like Play-Doh someone has just been fondling. Like a stress ball. Put it all in this squeeze, relieve the tension, harder, this is to save us! Harder! Use these muscles you often don't. Ignore the struggle, she's already gone and just doesn't know it yet...You had no choice, we must get help...the *right* kind of help...*our* kind of help.

Sudden acute awareness. Of the warmth of the light coming from the ceiling, of the way the air sits on the exposed skin, of her hands squeezing and rending. Of things tearing which should not. Sounds that can't be. Earless body, right hand third finger torn away like a trimmed plant, human fibers like gestures or fading smoke. She breaths upon the blood as she tries not to puke or faint and fall face-first into it, sees it shimmer and waver. Tears running down her face and the front of her shirt. *This isn't real—I didn't do this*—Hamburger spice and parts of starfish. Blood pulling away from her. Chest pulling away from her. *Run.*

Run. We can't stay here now. Let the gaps in your consciousness guide you. That voice, where is it coming from? That's not my voice! Run...like it says. Run.

chapter 13

face in the window. Too ghostly to be her own. Too scared and broken-looking. Like cracked clay or slick light from a fistula. Too etched with hurt. Translucent reflection riding the awnings and street-signs. People keep piling on. Yellow lights pop on. Katherine can't see her face anymore. For the best. Wet dog and feet smell, old B.O. cooped up with a cold. All the worst scents collecting in the warm-breath air of the bus, soaked into the turquoise and lavender cloth seats. Blurry, everything hazy edges, faces, bodies, mounds of flesh under piles of fabric, Katherine can't focus on anything in particular, more shapes and colors, lights and shadows, feeling too tired to shift her eyes from this unseeing. To her side, another figure moves in, blue shape and black lines. She recognizes the person in a vague sense from the blue of the pant-legs, the belt, the holster. The pistol grip peeking from it, the badge shimmering on the chest. The weary eyes, looking from passenger to passenger, searching for something to set the body into motion. Katherine thinks she smells the gun-oil over the wet asscrack and dollar-store perfume. She sees the light gleaming on the ridges of the pistol, the handle protruding from the black leather pouch, so shiny it looks wet, bulging from beneath some racy piece of lingerie, some sexy little teddy, some gimp suit. In her mind she could see the trigger, the barrel, shaft beneath cradle thongs. Lust in the lustre. Death in the insides. Coldness, the way the pieces of metal come together, hard finality. Katherine feels her breath growing ragged, growing quicker. Her body almost shivers beneath her clothing, electric wavering, muscles and montages of skin-covered cartilage. She feels like she is almost sizzling in the stuffy air. Was she turned-on? *That fucking thing...*Trying to shake the feeling but mostly unsuccessful, Katherine looks across the aisle and sees a woman holding an animal carrier on her lap. A cat sits just visible inside, staring out at Katherine. The animal narrows its eyes at her. Katherine hears it emit a low growl, throaty and watery, followed by a sharp hiss. Her eyes meet yellow flashes from within the cage. Headlights holding her rapt, calling her. The sounds of the bus gone, only the wash of yellow light from the animal carrier surrounds her. Thin streamers or beams pulling her in. She feels there will be some comfort there, wherever the beams are leading her. Rest, maybe. She feels very tired suddenly, as if each of her organs is pulling in a different direction, fighting each other for control. Her hand is moving, she can't feel the fingers as they stretch or the little bones in her knuckles, reaching, reaching. Where are the little sensations across her skin? Where is the air tickling the hairs as the limb moves? It is as if it is moving on its own, before her face. Where is this arm headed? This one which looks so much like her own? Grasping as if at straws in the distance, fingers waver, hover, near-closed, the black leather and metal of the cop's gun coming closer to the flesh in-motion, Katherine still can't feel the blood flowing in her veins, still feels the pull of the cat's stare from inside the cage. Still—WAIT!—

Her mind screams every noise it can think to make, tries to wake her body up, every bad song lyric and stored bits of math equations and useless Jeopardy trivia fact it can find. Every nerve jumps to life all at once, every pore and hair sending sensation rushing upward, washing her brain, too much information coming in now, after almost none—

STOP, STOP, MUST STOP—

She can feel the space between fingers again, feel the thin cotton shirt-sleeve brushing her

bicep—

STOP IT! YOU HAVE TO STOP IT NOW—

The woman with the cat is looking at Katherine, staring mutely, her mouth open a little, seeing what is happening, her brain still trying to process the image. Katherine's fingers reaching, the cop, unawares, looking at the back of the bus at a couple of teens huddled and whispering. He hasn't seen us yet, there's still time to stop—

The bus lurches, shrieks to a juddering stop, and Katherine takes this moment of disorientation to will her body to stand, to flee as quickly as she can. Through the yellow windows, as the bus starts back up, she sees the woman with the cat, staring out the window, scowling at her. She doesn't so much see the cat's yellow piercing eyes as feels them as the bus pulls away.

Her insides on the outside. In the hedges next to the bus-stop. Her face in the plant, bent prostrate, Katherine hears a voice from behind her. Stupid laughter, drunk-coating to the words floating toward her, dripping booze and bad cologne. Parts of "Hey, look at this chick, she' probably as fucked-up as we are! I think she's puking, dude!" Stupid pitterings of laughter again. Katherine can picture some idiot sexual gesture, the group laughing dumbly. She wipes her mouth, and turns to look at them. Three young men, boys really, in pseudo-dress shirts and shorts, a uniform of douche-baggery, hair spiky and generic, matching their faces matching their honking voices and laughs, probably matching their names. One of them approaches Katherine, a bit unsteadily. The reek of stale booze gets to her before he does.

"You Ok?" He asks, breathing heavily, the 'You' sounding somewhere closer to 'Shoe' or 'Chew.' "We saw you, uh, puking, and shit."

"I'm fine."

"Oh, 'cause, I was just...concerned, y'know? I just wanted to see if you, like, needed any help, or anything."

"Leave me alone," Katherine growls.

"I mean, you're like, by yourself, drunk, throwing up on the street, I figure, y'know, this girl, she might need—" Before he finishes, Katherine steps in and uppercuts him hard on the jaw, sending him reeling backwards. A strange, precise motion, the punch had happened before Katherine could even realize it was her fist doing the hitting. All of the bones shifted, the soft warm flesh of the boy's face wrapping around it slightly, like pizza dough or one of those containers of toy slime. He gives out a soft bleat, strange animal moan, eyes closed tightly at the pain and surprise. Katherine looks at her fist in shock, tries to move it of her own accord, and finally can, relaxing the balled extremity, feeling a surge of pain rush in. Between the knuckles and pieces of cartilage, ringing the shafts of tendons like vibrating pipes, like a trombone blowing. The man's friends are yelling in surprise as he stumbles back to join them, cradling his jaw and glaring at Katherine.

"Hey, you didn't have to be such a fucking bitch—" one of the friends begins, and Katherine feels her fist ball itself again, feels someone else taking control of her rage like weapon. She lets out a snarl, and begins toward the group. The boys shriek and take off running down the street, and Katherine forces her legs to stop. Her body suddenly deflates, the energy propelling it floods away through her pores, through her eyes, into the atmosphere. As her limbs and heart-rate slow, a low whisper begins at the back of Katherine's head again. Laughter and harsh language. Harsh even for a middle-schooler trying out the most offensive combinations of new curse-words they've picked up. Harsh even for a monster inside your head. Katherine suddenly has an idea. If she lets her body do the thinking, can the thing inside her take control? She isn't sure. Let her legs take her where she needs to go. Take her somewhere safer, for herself and others. Drown out the thing inside with other thoughts, swelling thoughts, stories and chunks of old memories. If we make ourselves think too much, can it have room to do any thinking of its own? If we toss away control, can anyone take it? Make it as lost and confused as we are.

After some trekking and as little thought as she can muster, she ends up in front of her mother's apartment complex. Katherine wrings her hands together, shakes her head vigorously. Keep control keep control.

Can't go there. Flight just flight.
But mother is so safe. So warm.
And the kitty...
No! Stop it! Run! Don't think just run!

Somehow, she is on campus. Somehow, everyone around her is off. Everything is broken like old glasses, like warbling cassettes. Katherine tries to find some place to be alone, but there are bodies everywhere. Constant movement, tweekers and fidget spinning. All the chairs, all the nooks and crannies of the library. The quiet study nooks of the science building. Kids playing Magic Cards in the student lounge. Nowhere to be alone, even this late at night. Nowhere safe.

Flesh detached from faces, flapping like there's wind but the hallway is still. Lights from the holes. Lights from where their skulls and mouths should be. Katherine's breathing turns quick broken chunks. It's all she hears, though the rays of colored light are so strong she can almost feel a noise humming off them. Every face in the hallway colors and lasers, jagged tufts of flesh like packaging, the shuddering of light weight falling on white-painted brick walls. Run, her mind screams. These are not faces anymore. *This is the moment the world breaks* some voice echoes in her head—

Gaps in the ground outside, the whipping of orange and yellow and red leaves in the hot-air vents, almost like flames. The grass gone, the air the flavor of sour grapes, of old beer bottles and rose hips, the sounds of things her mind isn't even sure it hears, isn't sure how to process, shrieks and the noises of collapsing metal, low thud of a thousand quick car crashes, moaning like family members in the fry.

All the eloquent symptoms of Armageddon, all this poetry of fear and death in her mind, all pieces of her screaming to get away from that awful voice whispering in her brain, and it still takes so much effort to keep her legs moving, to press on.

Snakes coil and wave across the sky, what's left of it, bugs, maggots as rain, like that tunnel scene in Willy Wonka that scared the shit out of her as a kid. But the sprinkling of wriggling droplets isn't just a projection on a wall. A movie in a family front room. It isn't staying inside the frames. Katherine feels the skin beneath her fingernails, oscillating shiver of parts of her own digestive tract working.

She walks. Not thinking about the walking, not thinking about the destination. Just walks.

A city virtually atrophied, organs lost actors, hollow sights. Memories of the places she passes waver across her brainscape, she lets them grow and swell before floating off, lets them take over as much space as they can. Past the park, the first place she'd smoked a cigarette with Janie, who lived in California now, hiding under the slide and almost throwing up after the second disgusting puff. In the distance the hotel with the purple lights running up the side, sometimes other colors for holidays or special occasions. Memory of the old video store, now just a chain coffeeshop. She used to wander the aisles for long stretches of time out of time, looking at the covers, imagining all the worlds behind them. Her mother would have to set a limit to ten movies, or Katherine would never have stopped picking out tapes that looked intriguing. Would have buried herself in them, black plastic tomb. The schlocky horror flicks, the classics, the technicolor and the shining faces on the covers of the musicals. Shot on video classics of low-brow stupidity. A whole aisle just for imported anime tapes, all the best motorcycle cyberpunks, the unnatural sprays of blood, the lightning backgrounds. The poor dubbing and the fuzzy white letters scrolling across the television screen. The documentary section, and that one Angela Davis tape Katherine checked out enough times she could have purchased it herself. She probably wore out the translucent strip of tape inside, all the times she re-watched the film, a moving portrait of one of her heroes.

So many objects and spaces hold memories Katherine had nearly forgotten. There is the mattress store, still there, still looking condemned, still looking like a front for drug dealings, or human trafficking. A flash of riding her bike with her father up this street, stopping for waffle cones at the little stand which was long since faded away, warmth of daylight, the echo of bike pedals and thumping tires, the cool breeze tinged with air from the water-front. These memories feel comfortable, like a blanket to wrap in, like a sunlight bath across her mind and the inside of her skull. Soothing, calming, a place to hide—

I wanna be the mighty King. Feel his mane a crown around my head. Hear his roar as my own. Feel it rumble through my guts and out through a mouth of snarling teeth. We run. We sleep through the daylight hours. We find the fresh meat. Rub our faces in it. Rub it across our bodies, communion of dead flesh. The meat represents our power, the warm ooze of blood our freedom. We are in control of this kingdom. Take the pieces and rub them everywhere. Let the scent embed itself in our skin. Present ourselves as presents to this King, yes rub the meat, yes, work it in like marinade, we must be presentable. We are loyal subjects we are here to serve ourselves to you, we are meat—

Katherine feels wetness on the back of her skull, reaches. Comes away palm full of blood and tissue, dim recognition, her own brain seeping from pores or a pulsing hole, leaking down her neck and back like a runny egg.

Blood on her shirt. Soft words around the inner folds of her ear, like a daydream, piercing her. Calling her. Whispered nothings from her own head. *Who do you think you are?* It asks. *Who are you trying to get away from?*

Pop like a bubble. Pop like a blood burst. Pop like a can cracking open. Suddenly, Katherine can see her surroundings again, suddenly the grey walls of a butcher shop come into focus. Suddenly she realizes she is hovering over the large trash can in the shop, digging through the detritus and the bloody pieces, rubbing chunks of discarded meat and gristle all over herself. The brain she thought was oozing from the back of her head was just a bloated chunk of pinkish fat, warm and sticky. Flies had heard the ruckus, smelled the party, come to investigate. The voice in Katherine's head still laughing, the voice mocking without words, flooding images into her mind. She shakes it away, runs, tries to leave the hideous little cooing behind to no avail.

She is losing herself.

What makes people feel human? She doesn't even know where to start anymore.

Pulse of clouds. Bones of electric lights. Old drywall. A body wearing her face, little more than a seed casing. She is bled like animal. She is almost done. She is every scene hopeless. This film doesn't end well for her. She is the wrong term, the scorn for blooming. For the padded manila life she led. Before. Down the hill, among the blossoms, fruit bread and the fable of life's porcelain faces.

She is a crumpled wrapper, she is almost lost to the wind, now...

Katherine doesn't realize she has fallen asleep again until she awakens, sharp pinches all over her body. She looks around and sees an unfamiliar alleyway, and a hoard of mangy-looking cats surrounding her. They have worked into a small circle around her, nibbling and tonguing her flesh her and there, finding bloody bits and stray chunks of meat-parts. Katherine screams and leaps up, sending some of the more skittish cats running, creating hissing puff-balls out of others, stretching and yowling and backing slowly away from her. Katherine feels a sharp pain in her head. She looks into a window next to her, and catches sight of something moving across her forehead. Something wiry and tweaking. A small shape, smaller than her little finger, and about as wide. Writhing beneath the skin of her forehead. She couldn't feel it, but in the phantasmagorical reflection she sees it perfectly. *Maybe this is another hallucination?* She looks over the rest of her body for any other strange movements or objects, when she sees the skin around her right ring finger begin to darken. It goes completely black, starless sky. It shrivels, as the rest of her hand and arm turn the color of a collapsed star. It travels up her arm, across her shoulders, and splits. It follows her shoulders to the other arm and begins traveling down it, but also makes a sharp turn and begins down her chest, her side, into her hip. The arm where it started shrivels completely, and the skin begins to crack and shatter, begins to peel right off the bone. The muscle is gone, just a purplish-black gunk left in the tubes of arms where they once sat attached. The rest of her body follows suit, slowly, painlessly. But the smell of rotting flesh hung over her, and the terror of it all clamped her mouth shut and her feet to the battered pavement. Katherine closes her eyes, begins counting. She still smells the scent of burning animal fibers and licking sloppy-rotten fruit, still hears strange skin-wrenching sounds. Katherine finally reopens her eyes, and her skin is back in place, is back to the look of real human flesh. Living flesh. She looks in the window again, and sees a slight hint of movement as something slinks away back beneath her hairline.

chapter 14

landing at the library. Only place left to think. No one will bother her among the old book smells and the homeless people using the computers. Among the teens hanging out, trying to sneak kisses down deserted aisles, trying to carve names into the empty tables. Kids trying to find the *Joy of Sex* or the *What is Happening to My Body* books to look at and snicker, trying to find obscure fantasy and science fiction tomes they've read about online among the dusty covers. Or lost in their own world, the screen of a phone or laptop, games or fb or some weighty article. All the zonked-out others. She can fit nicely among them.

Katherine drifts aimlessly across pages. All the same. All bullshit. She knew Dr. Rawling wasn't a quack, she had proof of that. Now she needs to find those videos everyone keeps talking about.

Down the tube, the dark web. No grand entrance or to-do, just a brief pop-up box like how dial-up used to have, a message telling her she was connected, and empty space. Find your own way, kid, no one will help you here. Face your fears alone. This is where the adults play.

Katherine has a handful of leads scribbled down on a scrap of paper, and begins going through addresses, slowly as the connection breaks itself into a thousand small packets of information, travels through computers in every country from Turkey to Tibet. Dead end after dead end greet her, broken links, empty pages. Ghost-end of the street. The occasional scam-page, attack-links. Accidentally finding a few unseemly porn pages. Holding back sick running up her esophagus, holding in stifled moans of horror, the bodies and the things people do to them. Stumbling through a haze of hate and racist forums, fundamentalist ideocracy, IED diagrams, 8-bit artwork, hacked credit card numbers.

One of the last links she has written down provides the treasure she seeks. Sublight and tunnels and new hopes. She finally finds a sparse page, no pictures, no header, just two links, bright blue and labeled *asbvgggggg 1* and *2*. She clicks the first link. Nothing happens for a long time, but the cursor twirls to let her know it isn't frozen. Katherine sits tensely, trying to leave thought in another part of her brain; just scroll over the fake wood-grain of the table, the scent of armpits lingering in the empty chair next to her. The sound of the mouth-breather in the next row trying to suck the old book smell out of the library and into his inflamed throat.

A video of a child's birthday party. A girl is opening presents, and the other kids are gathered around watching her. One of the kids looks visibly sick, and as a cat walks cautiously by the child suddenly leaps up onto the table, dives head-first toward the concrete the cat stands on. The kid is saved at the last second by an adult, and the other children all begin freaking out, screaming and crying. The jumping kid begins attacking the adult who saved him, and the person holding the camera drops it. The video stops as it hits the ground and goes black.

Tears form at the edges of her eyes. Kat clicks the second link. The second video begins playing, this one of a higher quality. The camera shows a lab, disorderly, trash and equipment covering every available table and counter space. A young man steps into the shot, wearing an immaculately clean lab coat and looking at a tablet. He picks up a vial from the counter, and looks back to the tablet, checking for something. Another man enters the frame, and Katherine immediately recognizes Dr. Rawling from the few pictures she had been able to find of him. His lab coat is covered in a number of different-colored stains, his hair longer and more disheveled than any of the pictures she'd seen, his face growing the first hints of a beard.

"Hand me that tape measure, Tim. C'mon, get the lead out. There. Now, hold it here—"

Dr. Rawling points to a portion of his forehead. The assistant looks confused. He hesitates before stepping toward Dr. Rawling.

"There, C'mon boy. C'mon. No, not like that, just hold it—"

Dr. Rawling's words become indecipherable, garbled and choked sputtering. He slaps the tape measure away from his head with a quick motion, and screams a carnivore scream as he leaps at Tim, knocking him over and sending the camera flying. It lands, still recording, a thin crack running across the picture now, the camera on its side, only capturing the lower halves of Dr. Rawling and Tim struggling on the ground, but it is clear what is happening. The sounds and the wet splashes of red mist tell Kat everything she needs to know.

The clip ends and Katherine can't summon the strength to move. Everything seeps out in a rush and a splash. She stares at the empty screen. In the bottom corner, an ad for six-pack abs flashes blue strobes. In the pixelated darkness, Kat sees shapes. She sees the thing inside her, crawling, slithering around inside her tubes and tissues. She sees her mother flash in the empty video box, the shaded figure of her father beside her. Shadows dance across both their faces. Someone laughs. Katherine wonders if it was her before she stumbles out of her trance-like state, closing the browser and standing up from the chair. She still hears faint whispers of laughter, and now she is certain it isn't coming from her.

"This won't stop," she says aloud, mostly to be certain it is her thought and no one else's, to make sure she even can still speak. Something agrees with her. Katherine has a flash of a solution, and the something stirs. No more laughter. Hot anger wells up from somewhere, not her heart or gut or mind. Another source, same passion, same tinge of fear. That had struck a nerve. Maybe just her own.

"Maybe we can make a deal." Katherine speaks. Eyes wide in horror. Hands shoot to cover mouth. Stop the sounds. Who put them there? Her voice on puppet strings. Katherine quickly jumps to an old song, lyrics washing her thoughts away like thick coats of neon paint.

"—Hey, look, why don't we just—" begins her mouth moving, in a voice completely hers, when she ceases singing. She begins the words again. This is it. This might just work...

Katherine sings, and for a moment, she is wonderfully alone.

chapter 15

was singing old lines from songs, poems, films to herself as she strides the tall aisles of the hardware store the only way to keep that other voice away? That gristly tone, the almost painful pitch of laughter. *"I leave this lullaby of tears."* Count the aisle numbers. Past Plumbing, past Lumber, past mock shower-stalls and the paint aisle. Past the aisle full of mirrors. Do you think it is just yourself being reflected? Finally coming to the aisle she needs. Number 11: power tools. Peruse the merchandise. Keep up the soft singing, it drowns out the other voice. *"Mommy always said there were no monsters or creatures or demons in the night, only human evil, but I think she's wrong."* Katherine tries to block out the things she sees, she hears. Masses of dots, exploding faces, some recognizable some strangers, all screaming. Quiet screaming no sound screaming. Fingers across the radio signals, coughing wet red phlegm through the windows. Katherine closes her eyes again against an almost indecipherable growling inside her head. Echoing the folds of her brain, traipsing across memories and motor functions. What if it changed her most cherished memories? Did something to her father's face? What was left of her mother? What if it altered the way she walked, or talked, or wiped her ass? The thing hissed a jet of laughter in response. *"Tender moments with a burnt-out cigarette. I'm dying to know what doesn't happen next. Your drunken kisses leave a bitter taste on my lips"* she whispers, cutting the other voice off. Press forward, pay the person, don't look at the snarling thing waving from the rafters for too long, pretend you don't see the blood dribbling to the floor, hear the little jello plops of it. Just get your stuff and get out before you lose it.

Blood thickening in barbecue sauce splotches on the floor already. Landry still and propped in the corner, Katherine had covered her with a blanket and she looks like something from an old basement, some harmless house item stored and forgotten and waiting to be rediscovered among the disintegrating VHS tapes and the mouse shit. The room smells of rubble and musk. Old toes.

The room is just a movie replaced with shadows. With fake furniture and people.

The room is a set and this is just another role she is in. Dizzying array of props, the lights above

flickering and throwing just the right shade. She begins speaking, the audience must get the monologue, must get the external projection of her thoughts. Her words are not the sounds she usually makes, are not her own. They echo horrible and beastly, like some hollow incantation or infomercial prattle. Her words seem insincere in the face of this moment, this scene. She looks around the stage, looks for the audience, find her camera, find her cue. If this was a Hollywood movie, she would have a trailer and make-up people and assistants to take care of the gritty details. If this was Hollywood, she would have found some other way to save herself than this. But this is not a film, the stage is nothing more than a bombed-out studio apartment. Overly expensive, filled with empty liquor bottles and cigarette butts roiling up out of ashtrays and unidentifiable detritus mingling in piles. She positions herself as comfortably as she can in a chair, knowing this may not be easy. Knowing it may not work. She's felt strange pulls and urges in all her pieces since she left the hardware store, feeling as if each part of her body was trying to talk her out of what she was doing separately, one at a time. Stomach first, mostly normal. Head was next, then heart. When her toes tried to stop her was when she began to take notice. Both lungs feel like they are yelling at her, her old appendix scare pulled as if to run away from the rest of her. Hair stirred, fingers lifted, breath jumped from mouth as quick as it could manage, her eyes were the last to attempt a coup, each pulling in a different direction, weeping to get her attention, rolling and crossing and closing to show her this is not a good idea. To try to talk her out of it.

Struggle to even plug the drill in. Shivers as defense. Body revolts. Not body, but the thing inside it. The thing pulling strings. The thing taking control. Not for long.

Aim the damaging event carefully, keep all your focus, fight the urge to stop, to miss, fight the screaming in your brain that is not your own. "How can you be sure this isn't all in your head?"

No, no, no, NO! Keep moving, we are almost there. The cold metal touches the forehead for just a second, pin-prick of pain, the screaming grows more frantic, more terrified. It comes out her mouth as some alien gurgle, moaning and screeching. The tip begins tearing into the skin, the flesh, the pain rising, careful, any miscalculation one way or the other could mean lights out. Could mean the end. Could mean this thing wins and that's it. The tip hits bone and a new wave of pain shoots through Katherine's face, running from the bridge of her nose to the back of her neck, icy and biting, little razor blades dragged through the curvature of her body, keep pushing, more force is needed now, through to the bone, keep pushing, the pain seems to be floating away somewhere far off, or perhaps that is Katherine, falling into a fragment, wet sides and broken edges, dark space surrounding—

Katherine suddenly pushes too far, through the hardness of skull and into the soft brain tissue beneath, and sensation spikes. Wavers. All emotions at once. All feeling happens in unison, brain stuck in cycle, BUT THAT'S MY MEMORIES, the screaming in her head that is not her own bubbles out slowly, she feels a thick substance running down someone's face, sees a finger reach up to it and come back neon green, like splatter movie green, like 90's boy's toys green, the Ninja Turtles she used to steal from her cousin and play with as a young girl. A quick pop, and the tube fades out. Sounds are still ringing around the world, but Katherine is cold and just wants to float. She is star meat, a constellation of blazing rust and battering Van Gogh swirls. Katherine manages to laugh weakly, though she cannot move most of the rest of her body. It isn't there. But neither is the laughter.

The quiet is soft like a cherished memory.

about the author

Kyle Wright is a Chicago-based writer, musician and visual artist. He has published the chapbooks *Videodrome* and *mindfuck* (*Really Serious Literature)*, and his work has appeared most recently in *After Hours Press*, *Subterranean Blue Poetry*, and *Bleached Butterfly.* He is Editor-in-Chief of the online literary journal *Abandoned Library Press*. He has surfed couches across Europe, lived on a mountain in Colorado, worked as a wedding DJ, and played folk music at old folks' homes. He lives with his partner and their cat, Chickpea.